NURSE FRO

Swept off her feet by handsome surgeon
Adam Brent, Staff Nurse Kirsty Macrae
leaves her home in the Highlands and
follows him to St Luke's in London—only
to discover that she's made a terrible mistake. For not only has Adam forgotten
her, but he's already engaged to someone
else . . . .

NURSE FROM THE GLENS

BY

ELISABETH SCOTT

MILLS & BOON LIMITED
15–16 BROOK'S MEWS
LONDON W1A 1DR

CHAPTER ONE

KIRSTY had never expected the hospital to be so big. And it was a busy, noisy place, London, she thought dismayed, setting her suitcase down.

For a moment her heart sank and she wished that she was back in Invertorridon, ready to go on duty in the old stone hospital that stood high on the hills, looking down on the quiet little Highland town that had been home for all her life. How could she ever have thought that she could live in a place like this, so far away from her own folks and the glens she loved?

'Can I help you, love? The main entrance is across there—all the patients have to check in at the desk.'

The hospital porter had come out of his little room. He was thin and almost bald, and not much taller than Kirsty herself, but his voice, strange as it sounded to her, was friendly, and there was a warmth in his blue eyes. He's just a wee bit like Hamish Macfarlane at the Post Office, Kirsty thought.

She smiled. 'I'm not a patient, thank you, I'm a new staff nurse,' she told him. 'Where should I be going?'

He pointed to a red-brick building half hidden by the bulk of the hospital.

'That's the nurses' home, love, and I'm Joe. I hope you'll be happy at St Luke's. Can you manage your case, or do you want to leave it? I can have it sent across for you.'

Kirsty held out her hand to him.

'I'm Kirsty Macrae,' she told him. 'And I can manage it, thank you.' She lifted her suitcase up again and began to walk across to the nurses' home.

Of course I can manage it, she told herself, and she knew that she didn't mean only the heavy suitcase. Have I not been wanting to come here all through the last year of my training, ever since Adam Brent told me about St Luke's, ever since he said I should come here to work?

But there would be time enough to think of Adam Brent. Right now, she had enough to do settling in and getting ready to start work tomorrow. It might have been better if she'd done as her mother suggested and come to London just a few days earlier, to give herself time before she had to start work. But suddenly, after all these months of wanting to leave Invertorridon, wanting to come to St Luke's, she had found that one thing she had never thought of was just how hard it would be— leaving the glen, and all the goodbyes that had to be said.

'But it's not the end of the world I've come to,' Kirsty reminded herself as she sat waiting for the home sister to come. 'I could just be getting on the overnight train any time I felt like it, and I would be home in the morning.'

The thought made her feel much more cheerful

and when home sister, small and plump and bright, came in she was able to return her smile of welcome.

'Well, Nurse Macrae, you must be tired after your journey,' Sister said, when she had finished taking down all the information she needed. 'Would you like a cup of tea right now or would you like to go up to your flat?'

'I would love a cup of tea,' Kirsty replied with feeling, 'but it's taken me longer than I thought it would to get here. Maybe I'll just go and get my unpacking done.' Sister stood up.

'You'll probably find one of the other girls there, in any case,' she said, 'and you can make tea for yourselves. Now, my dear, remember to come to me if you have any problems. Your uniforms are in your room, just check with the list that's there.'

The lift took Kirsty and her suitcase to the fourth floor, and to flat 409, which was to be her home here at St Luke's. She opened the door with the key sister had given her and went inside, a little relieved to find that she seemed to be the only one there.

There were three bedrooms. One, with the door open, was obviously hers, for her uniforms were set out on the bed. Another looked as if its occupant had left it in some haste and the third had the door closed, with a notice hung on the handle—Sleeping, Do Not Disturb.

Kirsty peeped into the tiny lounge and saw that there was a kettle, with a tea-caddy and a jar of coffee beside it. She switched the kettle on, having filled it at the small sink in the bathroom, and made herself a cup of tea. It was a nice wee flat, she thought appreciatively, remembering the rather bare rooms the student nurses had had at her own hospital.

But of course, she reminded herself with pride, I'm a qualified nurse now, and this is my own hospital, St Luke's.

'Hi—you must be Kirsty.'

Startled, Kirsty looked up at the girl standing in the doorway. She was wearing a blue track suit, a deep blue that was just the colour of her eyes. And her hair, Kirsty thought, was just like the beech trees in the glen when it was autumn.

Rubbing her eyes sleepily, she came over and sat down on one of the other chairs.

'When I wake up properly,' she said, with her eyes closed, 'I could use a cup of coffee, if you felt like being kind.'

Kirsty poured a cup of coffee and moved it nearer her flatmate.

'I hope I didn't wake you—you'll be on night duty,' she said with heartfelt sympathy.

The blue eyes opened.

'Night duty? No, this is my day off, but I was at a party last night—didn't get home till all hours. Thanks, Kirsty, I need this. Oh, I'm Jane.'

When she had finished one mug of coffee and started on another, Jane woke up properly. She told Kirsty about herself, and about their other flatmate, Andrea.

'She's on surgical with you,' Jane said. 'She's in her final year, that's why she's allowed to share with such exalted beings as two staff nurses like you and me! Oh—you did know you were on surgical, didn't you?'

Kirsty set her cup down carefully.

'I asked to be,' she replied, not looking at the other girl. 'I'm keen to get some more experience in a surgical ward. We didn't do a great deal that was out of the ordinary at Invertorridon. Anything really interesting was done at Inverness, or even in Edinburgh.'

Jane stood up and stretched. 'Well, you'll certainly get plenty experience here. I'm in theatres, so I know what's coming to you. But what made you choose Luke's? I mean, we're not as famous as Guy's, say.'

Kirsty was glad that she was already on her way to rinse out the two mugs, for she could feel warm colour flooding her cheeks.

'Oh, someone I knew vaguely once mentioned that this was a good hospital to work in,' she said, and she hoped that her voice sounded as casual as she had meant it to be.

'Oh, it is,' Jane agreed. 'Look, it isn't paradise, but no hospital is. We have some real bloody-minded sisters, and the current bunch of first-years don't look as if they'll ever make nurses, but by and large it's not too bad. I'm off for a quick jog around the park—see you later.'

A moment later she had gone, leaving Kirsty a little bewildered and quite certain that Jane was very different from any of her nursing friends in Invertorridon. Different, but—yes, I like her,

Kirsty decided, knowing that she was once again making a snap judgment on someone.

Andrea Johnson, who came in when she came off duty in the evening, was quieter and obviously hard-working, for she settled down to do some studying right away. But her welcome, although quieter, was as genuine as Jane's had been and Kirsty thought, with considerable relief, that perhaps it wasn't going to be too difficult, settling down here at St Luke's.

And early the next morning the familiar and reassuring sight of herself in uniform and the knowledge that she was now a qualified and an experienced nurse, gave her a degree of courage. She went to report for duty on Harding ward, the womens' surgical ward on the second floor of the big hospital. She was a little early, and in the duty room the day sister was just finishing taking over from the night sister.

'Morning, Staff,' the taller one said briskly, before turning back to confer again with the older woman.

Five minutes later the assembled day staff were all given a brief run-down on the night sister's report. Kirsty, listening to Sister Dawson's pleasant and professional voice, thought that she was lucky and this was going to be a good ward to work on.

'Mrs Morton in six, one of yesterday's theatre cases, is likely to need a catheter,' she said. 'I want a check on her intake and output over the next six hours. Miss Jones, in twelve, had a disturbed night.

We may have to consider asking doctor to query her sedative. Next to her, in bed thirteen, the intravenous therapy tissued and Sister Wood set up the drip again at four a.m., so the patient must be checked regularly.' She looked down at her notes. 'Yes, the girl we have in ten—that's the small side ward, Staff—had respiratory complications after her anaesthetic, and Sister Wood isn't too happy about her.'

She turned to Kirsty. 'Right, Staff Nurse Macrae, while the BP observations are being made I'll give you a quick run-down on the floor.'

Kirsty followed Sister Dawson around the two large wards and the six smaller ones that made up the womens' surgical floor, listening with interest and attention to everything she was told and making certain that she would know where she had to go and what she had to do.

'You haven't been qualified very long, Staff?' Sister Dawson asked, when they had finished.

Kirsty coloured. 'I did my final exams three months ago,' she said quickly, 'and I applied to come here while I was waiting for my results.'

Sister Dawson smiled. 'I like a newly-qualified staff nurse,' she said. 'You're at the stage where you're pleased to be qualified, but you're still willing to learn. Well—are you?'

'I hope so, Sister,' Kirsty replied.

'Right,' Sister Dawson said briskly. 'Check that theatre case in six, please, Staff, and then you can bring me the BP observations as soon as they're ready.' She looked at her watch. 'Doctors' rounds from ten on, so we have a lot to do before then.'

The familiar routine of the ward soon claimed Kirsty, but she found time, as she went briskly but unhurriedly about her duties, to have a word or two with each patient. All too soon it was almost ten and Sister Dawson began checking that each case was ready to receive her doctor or specialist.

Kirsty, busy in the duty room filling in patients' charts, couldn't help looking up as the different doctors came. There was Dr Graham first, tall and white-haired, and then there was Mr Brown, who was small and obviously quick-tempered. Then a young doctor, whose name she didn't hear as Sister Dawson took him to the ward, and finally Dr Willett.

But no Adam Brent.

He was, she knew, a junior surgical registrar—so surely he would have cases on this ward? Kirsty longed to ask someone, but it wasn't the sort of thing a very new staff nurse could easily ask the ward sister.

She might, she thought, ask Andrea, if they went to lunch together, but the younger girl was off for first lunch and Kirsty for second, so there was no chance. She would do it, she decided, very casually—as if it didn't really matter to her. Perhaps back at the flat, in the evening.

But at the end of the day, when the day staff handed over to the night staff, Kirsty knew that she had to get away from the hospital—just to breathe, she thought. Sometimes she felt like this at the end of a busy and demanding day, much as she loved her work.

At home, in Invertorridon, she often used to come off duty, get on her old bike and cycle out into one of the glens that were so near the little town. And somehow, with the heather-covered hills to look at, and the green of the trees, and the distant sound of a burn gurgling its way through the glen— then she would feel at peace with herself and with her work. But here, in the heart of a busy city, with the glens so far away . . . What will I do, Kirsty thought, dismayed, when I'm feeling like this?

She remembered, then, that Jane had mentioned a park. Not really what she wanted or what she needed, but better than nothing. Joe at the gate told her that the park entrance was just along the road and Kirsty, her cloak wrapped around her, for there was a sudden chill in the breeze, made her way to it.

Not a very big park, but quite a bonny one, she decided a little later, with its trees, and its grass and the wee pond that would likely, in the summer, have children sailing boats on it. And peaceful, more peaceful than she would have thought possible in the centre of the city.

She sat down on one of the park benches, conscious now that her feet were very tired indeed. In this corner, out of the wind and with the afternoon sunshine on her face, if she closed her eyes she could almost think that she was back in the glen. Back in the glen, and Adam Brent beside her.

Kirsty closed her eyes and gave in to the memories.

Adam Brent had come to Invertorridon for a month at the end of last summer as a locum for old Dr Fraser, who had been Kirsty's family's doctor for all of her life. It was Dr Fraser who had encouraged her determination to be a nurse.

Dr Brent—Adam—had been at the farm one Friday afternoon when Kirsty had gone home for her weekend off. Her mother had had bronchitis and Kirsty had arrived to find the young doctor having a cup of tea with his patient at the kitchen table.

'Kirsty, this is Dr Brent. He's here while Dr Fraser has his holiday,' her mother had said.

But Kirsty had had no thought for anyone else, right then.

'And what's wrong with you, that you needed the doctor?' she asked severely.

'Just a wee touch of bronchitis, and it's just about better,' her mother replied. But she coughed, and Kirsty's eyes flew to the doctor's face.

'It's all right, Kirsty,' Adam Brent said, understanding her anxiety. 'She really is almost clear, and I'm sure you'll see that she behaves herself.'

'I certainly will,' Kirsty promised.

He had risen to go then, saying he would look in the next day as he would be near the farm in any case. And the following day Kirsty had walked to the car with him, answering his questions about the local hospital and listening as he talked about the post he hoped for as junior surgical registrar at St Luke's.

Somehow, over the few weeks he was in Invertorridon, he got into the habit of dropping in at the farm if he was anywhere near. Kirsty herself wasn't always there, but when she was, she enjoyed talking to the tall young doctor with his eyes as dark as his hair. And sometimes when he didn't have too many visits to make, they would climb the hill behind the farm and sit leaning against one of the big fir trees at the top, talking of the work they both loved.

'There just isn't enough time,' Adam Brent said once, his dark eyes serious, concerned. 'Don't you often feel, Kirsty, that you need more time to spend with your patients, to get to know what's troubling them as well as what their medical problems are? Time to learn all you need to know to be able to care for them properly.'

It was a strange feeling for Kirsty, having her unformed thoughts put into words like that.

'Yes, I do feel that,' she replied slowly, wonderingly. 'And here in Invertorridon I wonder sometimes if I'm getting the chance to learn all I should. Oh, I pass my exams all right and I know about the things I'm supposed to know in theory, but I think it would be better if I could be nursing some of the people with textbook names for their troubles!'

Adam smiled, and Kirsty thought afterwards that that was when she began to realise what was happening to her.

'Don't be impatient, Kirsty,' he said. 'Do your

finals, get your qualification, and then you can really start learning. Maybe you should do what I'm doing—come to St Luke's once you're through. It's not the top, I know, but I enjoyed my time there as an intern and I think the world of Frank Graham. He'll be my chief if I get this job.'

'I hope you do get it, Adam,' Kirsty said earnestly. And all at once there was a small, cold feeling around her heart at the thought of him going in such a short time.

A week before he left he heard that the post was his and he came out to the farm to tell the Macraes. Kirsty's mother insisted that he stayed to have tea with them and Kirsty left her studying, knowing there was so little time left, to go for a walk up the glen with him before he went.

'I'm sorry you and I have never worked together, Kirsty,' Adam said the day before he left. 'I think you must be a good nurse.'

'I hope so,' Kirsty replied, not quite steadily. She wondered if he would ask her to write to him, but he didn't. But of course, she told herself quickly, he knows that I have my studying to do and he knows that he is to be working very hard.

'Goodbye, Adam,' she said when they parted.

'Goodbye, Kirsty—and don't forget, think about coming to St Luke's when you're through,' he told her.

For a moment she thought that he would kiss her, but he didn't. And after he had gone, she told herself that Adam was not the kind of man to be rushing things. He had said that she should go to work at his hospital, at St Luke's, and—and here I am, Kirsty told herself as she sat in the park with the sun warm on her face.

Here I am, working at St Luke's, and before long I will be seeing Adam. And I wonder what he will do and what he will say when he sees me again.

CHAPTER TWO

'WELL, well, if it isn't one of Miss Nightingale's young ladies!'

The deep voice, warm with laughter, made Kirsty's eyes open, startled. She sat up, straightening her cap automatically, and looked indignantly at the tall young man standing looking at her.

'And who do you think you are,' she asked him, 'that you can just—just come up and give me a fright like that?'

'I'm sorry,' he said, not sounding at all sorry. 'I'm Mike Wilson—I saw you in the canteen today. But I shouldn't have spoken without letting you know someone was there. You might have had a heart attack, mightn't you?'

In spite of her indignation, Kirsty couldn't help returning his warm and friendly smile.

'That's much better,' he assured her. 'That was quite a fierce scowl for a little thing like you!'

Warm colour flooded Kirsty's cheeks, for her lack of height had always been a sore point with her.

'I'll have you know,' she told him coolly, 'that little or not, I'm a fully-qualified nurse.'

His blue eyes studied her. 'Not very long qualified, I'd take a bet,' he said thoughtfully. And then, before Kirsty could take offence at this, he added disarmingly, 'I bet you've been a nurse just about as long as I've been a doctor—a few months! But it feels good, doesn't it?'

'It does indeed,' Kirsty agreed.

'If it hadn't been for your uniform I'd have thought you were a first-year student nurse,' he told her. 'In the canteen today you looked so small and so young, and rather as if you thought someone might come and take you back to school any moment!'

'I know,' Kirsty replied sadly. 'I suppose it's because I'm wee. But it's a sore trial to me, I can tell you, people thinking I'm not old enough to be qualified. I'm twenty-one, actually.'

'And a very pretty twenty-one, at that,' the young doctor murmured, and Kirsty was suddenly very conscious of her soft brown curls escaping from the knot that had started the day off so neatly, and the freckles that were probably all too visible on her small nose.

'I'll have to go,' she said hastily, and she stood up. The young doctor stood up as well.

'I'll walk back across the park with you,' he offered, and without giving her a chance to refuse, he turned with her. 'What ward are you on, Kirsty?' he asked.

'Harding,' she told him.

'Like it?' he enquired.

'Yes, I do,' Kirsty said after a moment. 'But this was my first day and it's quite a bit different from the hospital I trained in.'

Because he really did seem interested, she told him about Invertorridon and the hospital, about her training and her decision to apply for a job at St Luke's once she had qualified.

And then, very casually, before she could lose her courage, she said, 'Actually, last year one of the doctors from St Luke's came to Invertorridon as a locum—he said it was a good hospital to work in.'

'Oh? Who was that?' Mike Wilson asked with interest, and Kirsty was glad of the dusk and the sounds of traffic from the road which made it a little easier for her to speak lightly.

'Adam Brent,' she told him. 'I think he was waiting to hear whether he'd actually got the post here—as junior surgical registrar.'

'Brent?' Mike repeated. 'Brent? Oh yes, of course, I know who you mean. I haven't come across him myself yet, but I believe he's very good. I've heard that old Graham thinks highly of him.'

'I saw Dr Graham today,' Kirsty said, still lightly, she hoped, 'on his ward rounds. But Dr Brent wasn't with him.'

'Probably doing a round on his own, across in Newton—that's male surgical,' Mike replied just as casually. 'No, I did hear his name mentioned the other day. I think someone said he's off at a conference in Edinburgh—quite an honour apparently, at this stage.'

And just yesterday, Kirsty thought, there I was in Edinburgh with all that time to spare, waiting for the night train and never thinking that Adam was there. Not that it would have made any difference, she reminded herself hastily, for he would have been busy with his conference. And there would be time enough when he came back to St Luke's.

Now she was really glad that she had met this friendly young doctor, and she smiled at him as they reached the hospital gate and held out her hand.

'It was nice meeting you, Mike,' she said, 'even if you did give me such a fright, and me sitting peacefully there! Goodbye.'

'Hey—wait a minute, Kirsty,' he protested.

Gently but firmly, Kirsty reclaimed her hand.

'My room-mates will be thinking I'm lost,' she told him. 'Bye.'

At the corner of the nurses' home she turned and waved. Mike, still standing looking a little surprised, waved back.

I suppose, Kirsty thought, smiling a little, a good-looking young man like that isn't accustomed to a girl hurrying away from him. For he certainly was a good-looking man, and him with those deep blue eyes and his hair so fair against the brown of his skin. Yes indeed, a fine looking young man, Kirsty thought with untouched admiration. Perhaps many people might think him better looking than a dark, serious fellow like Adam Brent.

Perhaps—but not me, Kirsty decided, as she went into the flat on the fourth floor. It was a pleasant surprise to find that Andrea was waiting for her to come home so that they could go down to supper together, and Kirsty was glad to have the quiet student nurse with her as they went into the nurses' dining-room.

'I'm sorry I was so long coming,' Kirsty murmured. 'Are we very late?'

The big dining-room looked almost empty, apart from a group of nurses at one of the small tables.

'It doesn't matter,' Andrea assured her. 'The dining-room's open for another hour because people come off duty at different times.' She smiled, and Kirsty saw a touch of mischief behind the shyness. 'And of course, people like Jane have such a busy social life when they're off duty that *they* come in at all hours!'

It was a pleasant dining-room and Kirsty like the small tables with red-checked table-cloths. The food was good, too, and later, back in their flat, while Andrea was studying, Kirsty wrote to tell her mother and father all the details she knew they would want.

'Especially my mother,' she told the younger girl later, when she took her a cup of tea. 'She'll be delighted to hear that I had a good plate of soup, and very tasty cottage pie and salad, and a bowl of milk pudding!'

Andrea took her glasses off. 'She sounds like my mother,' she agreed. 'Thanks for the tea, Kirsty— I've almost finished for tonight.'

Somehow, when Kirsty went on duty the next morning, Harding ward already looked and felt familiar to her. She checked the catheter for Mrs Morton but before she went back to report to Sister

Dawson, she saw that the woman in the bed needed more than just medical observation.

'What about afterwards, Nurse?' Mrs Morton asked, unsteadily. 'Will I—will everything work as it should?'

'Everything will work just fine, Mrs Morton,' Kirsty told her. 'You know it's a big operation, a hysterectomy, and it's not surprising that some of the rest of your body gets a wee bit of a shock at it all. Now all we're doing with this catheter is giving you time to get back to normal after the operation. I'm fairly sure that sister will say it can come out tomorrow.'

'Sister might even say that later today,' Sister Dawson said from the doorway and Kirsty turned round, apprehensive until she saw the slight smile of approval in the older woman's eyes. 'Staff Nurse, I'd like to go over the drug cupboard procedure with you, you will have to take over any time I'm not here.'

This was no problem for Kirsty, for at the hospital at home they had been so short-staffed that for most of her final year she had in fact been given many of the responsibilities of a Staff Nurse. So she was well accustomed to the formalities that had to be strictly adhered to in the administering of drugs to patients.

When Sister Dawson had finished she turned to Kirsty. 'I liked the way you talked to Mrs Morton, Staff,' she said quietly. 'That was just what she needed. Yesterday she was too woozy from the anaesthetic to worry about what we were doing, but she's obviously had time to think about it now.'

And thank goodness, Kirsty thought with relief, that Sister Dawson isn't one of those sisters who believe that a nurse shouldn't even pass the time of day with a patient! For if she had been, I don't think she and I would have got on too well together!

The rest of the day flew by in the busy hospital routine. This surgical ward, running at full capacity, was a very different place from the surgical wards Kirsty had known during her training. As she had told Adam Brent, the local hospital had been fairly limited in its surgical cases. Tonsilectomies, appendicectomies, a hernia or two, and not much more, Kirsty had often thought.

On Harding she was already nursing two hysterectomy patients, one mastectomy, and three who had had arterial operations. It was hard work with the ward as full as this, but she didn't mind for she loved it and already she was beginning to get to know some of the patients. By the third day she came back from lunch to be told by Andrea that Mrs Morton had said she wanted her injection from the little Scottish nurse, because she did it so that you hardly felt it!

Jane, her pretty red-haired flat-mate, had invited both Kirsty and Andrea to go with her to a party. Andrea had refused pleasantly but firmly, saying that she had studying to do. Kirsty hesitated, feeling that she didn't really want to get into the social party-going set Jane obviously enjoyed, but at the same time unwilling to hurt the other girl's feelings.

'Of course you'll come, Kirsty,' Jane told her.

'It's just round the corner from the hospital. My friend Sally has a flat in that big block beside the park. You'll like Sally—she's mad, you'd never think she came top in our exams last year, but great fun. She's in casualty now.'

As she often did, Kirsty felt quite breathless with Jane and somehow she found that she seemed to have agreed to go to the party.

'I'm not really a party girl,' she told Jane two nights later, as they made their way along from the hospital.

'Then it's time you had a taste of being one,' the other girl replied. 'I couldn't survive a day on the wards without knowing I was going to do something pretty exciting later. Theatre isn't quite as bad, but I certainly couldn't just sit around and read and knit!'

Kirsty laughed, for she neither could *she* see this tall, slim redhead, always on the go, always rushing off somewhere, always coming home late, sitting down quietly and knitting.

'I find being on Harding quite exciting,' she said mildly, but Jane only shrugged.

Kirsty didn't think she had ever seen quite as many people all in one fairly small room. The music was loud and some of them even seemed to think there would be room enough to dance. As soon as they were inside, Jane was claimed by a tall young doctor Kirsty recognised from the ward rounds. Although, she thought, he had looked quite different then, in his white coat and following respectfully a few paces behind the quick-tempered specialist, Mr Brown. Now, in jeans and a casual shirt, he looked anything but studious and respectful as he and Jane danced in the crowded room.

Kirsty, abandoned, was wishing fervently that she hadn't come when a voice called her name.

'Kirsty—don't move! I'm coming!'

It was Mike Wilson, and Kirsty couldn't help a stab of relief at the sight of even one face she knew.

'This is a bit of luck,' Mike said breathlessly as he reached her. 'Here I was, wondering how I was to find you again short of risking Sister Dawson's wrath by creeping up to the ward, and here you are! Who did you come with?'

'Jane,' Kirsty told him. 'Jane Farrant, the red-haired girl over there.'

'Oh, I know Jane,' Mike said airily. 'If I'd known you were a friend of Jane's I would have known how to find you. You haven't got anything to drink—I'll get you a glass of wine.'

When he returned and handed her a glass of wine, his hand covered hers for a moment as he gave it to her.

'Are you sure, now,' he asked her, his voice warm and teasing, 'that Miss Nightingale would allow her young ladies to have a glass of wine? Especially one of her young ladies who's come all the way from the glens of Scotland!'

Kirsty didn't want to rise to his teasing but she couldn't help herself. 'I'll have you know, Dr Wilson,' she told him, 'that you just might be a wee bit surprised if you were to come to one of the ceilidhs in the glens—around Invertorridon, at least! Many a grand party I've been to. Different from this one perhaps, but a merry party right enough!'

Mike Wilson shook his head. 'You're different from any girl I've ever met, Kirsty Macrae,' he told her. 'Come on, let's enjoy this merry party right here!'

She hadn't thought it possible for one more couple to find room for dancing, but somehow they did, and although the dancing was not quite the kind Kirsty had been accustomed to, she found that she could pick it up quite easily with Mike Wilson's blue eyes laughing down into hers and his arms holding her close.

Once, when he left her to push his way through the crowd to get some more wine, Jane left her partner and came across to Kirsty.

'Kirsty,' she said, breathlessly, 'I see you're with Mike Wilson. Just watch him, that's all.'

'Watch him?' Kirsty repeated, puzzled.

Jane nodded her shining red head. 'Watch him,' she said darkly. 'I doubt if there's a student nurse in the hospital who wouldn't tell you exactly what I mean! And I know you're old enough to look after yourself, but I just felt I'd better give you a word of warning.'

Even in the warm room, Kirsty could feel her cheeks grow warmer.

'Thanks, Jane,' she said, above the hubbub of noise, knowing she couldn't take offence at her room-mate. 'But you don't need to worry about me, really.'

Because I'm not in any danger from any of his ploys, she thought as Mike reached her again. Och, an evening like this is fun, and a lad like Mike is great to be out with, but he's not for me.

An hour later, she found it wasn't quite as easy to convince Mike Wilson of that. She had accepted his offer to run her back to the nurses' home in his car because it had started raining, and having done that, she realised, she shouldn't have been too surprised when he stopped round at the back door instead of the front.

'Goodnight, Mike,' she said quickly. 'Thank you for bringing me back, I'll just be—'

'Oh no you won't, my girl,' Mike replied, laughter in his voice. 'Come here.'

The next moment his lips were on hers, his arms were holding her close to him, and—

'Just you stop that this minute, Mike!' Kirsty said severely. 'I'm not having any nonsense from you.'

Taken by surprise, he did stop. 'But Kirsty—' he began.

'*But Kirsty* nothing,' she said, and she sat up straight. 'If we're to be friends, you and I, we'll just get this clear at the start. I don't mind a goodnight kiss, but I'm not being pawed around. You'll just be keeping your hands to yourself. Is that clear?'

It was a moment before he could reply.

'Yes, I think it is,' he said, and then he was silent again. Just as Kirsty was thinking that she had lost his friendship and regretting this just a little, he burst out laughing. 'I said you're quite a girl,

Kirsty, and I was right. OK—that's clear! But we'll have to seal it with a kiss.'

She looked at him doubtfully. But he took her in his arms and kissed her very thoroughly and very pleasantly.

'Goodnight, Kirsty,' he murmured, his lips still close to hers. And then, laughter in his voice again, 'And I promise I'll be a good boy!'

'You'd better be,' Kirsty told him, but she couldn't help smiling as she got out of the car and went into the nurses' home.

She was glad that the following day was her day off and she didn't have to be on duty before seven. The day passed pleasantly with a bit of shopping, washing her hair, knitting and reading, but she wasn't sorry to have only one day off and to be back on the ward again. Surely, she thought, it couldn't be long now before Adam Brent returned from the conference and joined the other doctors on ward rounds. .

Two days later he was there.

He had passed with the other doctors before she looked up and, even in his white coat and with his head half turned, she knew him right away. But he looked different somehow, here on the ward, from the Adam she remembered in the glen.

It wasn't easy to go on writing up the reports as she was supposed to be doing, knowing that he was so near, knowing that soon she would see him. But Kirsty forced herself to finish what she had to do and then sit, waiting, until the doctors were on their way out of the ward. Fortunately, she realised,

Sister Dawson wasn't with them and Adam was a little behind the others.

She went to the door of the duty room. 'Dr Brent,' she said, quite softly, just as he was passing.

He stopped, and looked down at her. 'Yes, Nurse?' he asked, and Kirsty, all at once not caring who might see her or hear her, put her hand on his arm.

'Hello, Adam,' she said, smiling.

He looked down, his dark eyes remote. 'Did you want something, Nurse?' he asked, formally.

And Kirsty, appalled and shaken, saw that he obviously couldn't even remember who she was.

CHAPTER THREE

AFTERWARDS, Kirsty could have died with shame every time she remembered Adam Brent looking at her with polite interest—and no recognition at all. And she could do nothing but stand there outside the duty room looking at him, wishing with all her heart that she had stayed in the glens, that she had never left the familiarity and the safety of the hospital at Invertorridon.

Then, when it seemed to her that she had been standing here locked in this dreadful embarrassment for all her life, the coolness left Adam's dark eyes and he was smiling at her.

'Kirsty!' he said. 'Kirsty Macrae—how nice to see you.' He glanced at her cap. 'And qualified, too, I see. Congratulations!'

'Thank you,' Kirsty replied, and she hoped that she was managing to return his smile.

'How is your mother?' Adam asked then. 'And your father? Do give them my regards when you write.'

'I'll do that,' Kirsty said, her voice as polite as his.

She turned to go back into the duty room, wanting nothing more than to be alone, away from this man she had dreamed of and longed to see for all these months, but Sister Dawson came out of the ward and stopped when she saw them.

'You should be thanking me for your new Staff Nurse, Sister,' Adam Brent said lightly, pleasantly. 'I did some recruiting for St Luke's when I did that locum in Scotland last year. I told Kirsty, Nurse Macrae, that she should consider coming to St Luke's once she was qualified.'

For a moment the older woman's eyes rested on Kirsty thoughtfully, and Kirsty forced herself not to look away.

'I'm certainly grateful to you, Dr Brent,' Sister Dawson replied. 'Nurse Macrae does have the makings of a good nurse. Dr Brent, I'm glad I caught you—there are a few things Mrs Morton wants to ask you before she leaves hospital and she didn't want to say anything until she got you on your own.'

'Certainly,' Adam Brent said, turning back with her. 'I'll be seeing you, Kirsty—keep up the good work.'

Kirsty nodded, all at once unable to speak, and turned back into the safey of the duty room, glad to sit down at the desk and busy herself with the reports. And she was grateful, as the day went on, for the busy hospital routine and for the full ward that meant she was too occupied to think, too concerned with all that had to be done, to remember that awful moment.

All too soon it was lunch-time and the trolleys had arrived from the kitchen. Sister Dawson, obviously relaxed about Kirsty's ability to take charge, had gone off for her own lunch and Kirsty checked the diet list, making certain that the patients who had had arterial operations were given a low-cholesterol diet, those who had had intestinal operations were given a low-residue diet, and soft diets for patients who had had abdominal operations. Then there were two diabetics and a few who were still only on liquids.

Mealtimes were always busy, but Kirsty didn't mind. As she worked, as she moved from bed to bed, making certain that each patient could cope with her food, she knew that just around the corner of her mind there was the bleakness of the knowledge that she would have to face up to before long. But not yet, she thought, not yet, as she hurried along the corridor to answer an insistent bell from one of the side wards.

And then the day was over, the new shift had come on and it was time to leave the brightly-lit and busy hospital, time to go back to the flat. Time to stop running, Kirsty knew. All at once she couldn't bear to go over to the nurses' home and up to the little flat she shared with Jane and Andrea. She liked them both, but Jane, in spite of her whirl of social life and her constant rushing from work to play, was very perceptive. Kirsty had the uneasy feeling that Jane's blue eyes would see right through her defences and know that something had happened. And if she said anything, both Jane and Andrea would be sympathetic—sympathetic, but also curious, and Kirsty knew she couldn't bear that.

Without really thinking about it, she walked out

of the hospital gates and across to the park. What she wanted and needed were her own heather-clad hills, her own glens, the peace and the solitude that she had always loved, to soothe her aching heart and ease the tightness that she was now conscious of in her throat. But Invertorridon and the glens were far away and she would have to settle for a quiet corner of a park in London and be grateful that, because it had been raining earlier, there were few people around.

Now there could be no more pushing away the memory of that moment when Adam Brent had looked at her and she had seen that he couldn't think who she was. Oh, he had remembered, and recognised her, and probably it hadn't taken as long as it had seemed to her. But there was no getting away from the truth.

And the truth was, Kirsty thought bleakly, that while she had been working towards coming here, dreaming of seeing him again and longing for the moment when they would meet, Adam Brent had in all probability not given her one thought from the time he left Invertorridon until today.

Sitting in the park with her cloak drawn around her and her small, capable hands clasped together, Kirsty remembered the first operation she had seen, remembered how the surgeon's scalpel had seemed to probe the wound. Now she forced herself to do the same, no matter how painful it was.

She thought over everything Adam Brent had said to her when they had been together in Invertorridon. She forced herself to remember not only his words but how he had said them, the way he had looked at her, the expression on his lean brown face, in his dark eyes.

And at last, painfully, achingly, she admitted to herself that he had never, in fact, said or done anything to make her think that there was more between them than friendship. And a brief friendship at that, she reminded herself. Out of sight, out of mind, you could say.

But gradually the bitterness left her, because Kirsty was a fair-minded girl and she knew that she had no right to feel bitter. She knew that she had made much more of what Adam Brent had said than he had ever meant her to. And that, Kirsty said to herself with a revival of her usual spirit, was my fault, not his!

Somehow, once she had reached that stage, she began to feel a little better and her usual resilience took over, helping her to see things in a more positive light.

After all, she thought, I'm doing a job I like, I'm getting excellent training, and I will see Adam from time to time on the ward and around the hospital. He did seem quite pleased to see me, once he remembered me, and we did get on well. We enjoyed talking about work, about patients; we found that we thought the same way about so much in medical work. You never know! I'm going to work hard, I'm going to enjoy myself. I'm going to be realistic about Adam Brent, but I'm not giving up hope!

And with that extremely positive thought, she

realised that the rain had started again and she got up and hurried back across the park, along the road, and over to the nurses' home, feeling very much better than the sore-hearted Kirsty who had come in.

That same positive attitude made her decide, a few days later, to accept Mike Wilson's fairly casual invitation to come out one evening for a pizza and to see a film. They were both on duty late, so they went to the film first and then for their pizza.

Jane had warned Kirsty again, when she heard who she was going out with, but Kirsty had reassured her that she could manage Mike. And that young man certainly seemed to have accepted what she had said to him. He was fun to be with and she couldn't help but laugh at some of the outrageous stories he told her about the people at the hospital.

'I don't believe you, Mike,' she protested, laughing at his tale of the correct and impeccable Dr Sharpe being caught in the broom cupboard with one of the student nurses.

'Gospel truth, I swear it,' Mike assured her, earnestly. 'If you don't believe me, ask Sister Haines. She was the one who found them!' He cut some more of the large pizza and put it on her plate in spite of her protests. 'Come on, Kirsty, a wee thing like you needs building up—I'm just sorry it's not haggis.'

'I'm not,' Kirsty told him truthfully. 'I'm sorry if you think that north of the border we spend all our time eating haggis and dancing Highland flings, but I don't like haggis and I haven't danced a Highland fling since I was ten years old and at dancing classes!'

The young doctor threw his head back and laughed.

'I do like you, Kirsty Macrae,' he told her. 'You're different from any other girl I've known.'

When he took her back to the nurses' home he kissed her goodnight, a kiss that was expert and extremely thorough, Kirsty had to admit breathlessly. But a kiss that stuck to the rules she had given him.

'You see?' he murmured, his lips still close to hers. 'I said I would behave, didn't I?'

'You did that,' Kirsty agreed, smiling.

'So will you come with me to this hospital do next week?' he asked her. 'It's a cheese and wine thing and there'll be some speeches to mark the opening of the new wing. We're all supposed to turn up. I wasn't looking forward to it, but it will be all right if you come with me.'

Kirsty said that she would, knowing, as she agreed, that her first thought had been that perhaps she would see Adam there. That would be more satisfactory than the brief glimpses she had of him as he did his ward rounds.

She went on enjoying the work on the ward and there was no doubt, she thought as the days went by, that she was learning many new aspects of nursing. There was so much that she could never have learned in the limitations of the hospital at Invertorridon.

Apart from emergencies, Tuesday was operating

day for the ward and the routine and arranged operations were always scheduled for then. The theatre list was carefully planned and it was up to the staff of Harding ward, as well as the theatre staff, to see that the whole procedure ran smoothly.

Kirsty found her first operating day became a blur as she tried to keep on top of all that had to be done, getting patients down to theatre, preparing those who were about to go, hurrying down in response to calls that patients who had been operated on were ready to be brought back to the ward. There had never been anything like this pressure during her training, she thought breathlessly more than once.

But somehow, by the next operating day, she was able to cope with the demands made on her. There were the necessary preparations to be made for each patient, depending on the operation to be done. Then there were the pre-meds, the injection to be given about an hour before the patient would be wheeled down to theatre, so that by that stage she would be drowsy and relaxed, ready for the theatre staff, the anaesthetist and then the surgeon to take over.

And while one patient was in the theatre, Kirsty and the rest of Harding staff would be preparing the next patient, giving the next pre-med, checking that no patient who had had a pre-med was out of bed, and then on hand to take the lift to theatre. On their return they brought patients back to the ward, along with any special post-operative instructions.

Kirsty, bringing back a patient who had had an ulcer operated on, had to pass on to Sister Dawson what the theatre sister had said.

'They kept Mrs Jones longer in the recovery room,' she reported, 'because her blood pressure dropped to seventy-forty during the operation. It's now at eighty-fifty, Sister says.'

Sister Dawson nodded.

'Thank you, Staff,' she said briskly. 'You know the procedure, of course—half-hourly checks for the next four hours. I'll come with you now. We'll speed up the normal saline drip and raise the bottom of the bed—Trendellenberg position.'

By the time this was done Kirsty had to give a pre-med to Mrs Loxton, who had a lump in her breast. Mrs Loxton had been bright and cheerful the night before, and she was still sitting up in bed, lipstick on, her hair carefully done, when Kirsty reached her. But Kirsty, drawing the curtains around the bed, saw the brightness fade and the fear in the woman's eyes.

'I'm sure I don't know what the fuss is all about, Nurse,' Mrs Loxton said, not quite steadily. 'It's just a little lump after all, and here they are, making me sign a paper to say that they may have to—they may have to—'

She stopped, unable to put it into words. And Kirsty, with the hypodermic syringe ready in her hand, stopped too.

'Doctor explained to you, Mrs Loxton,' she said, her voice steady, reassuring. 'What they're going to do is take a small piece of the lump, and analyse it.

If everything is all right, they'll just remove the lump. If they find that the lump is malignant, then—'

'Cancer, you mean,' the older woman broke in.

'Yes, I mean cancer,' Kirsty said steadily. 'If it is, they will want to go right ahead and remove as much as is necessary. I promise you, Mrs Loxton, they will do no more than is necessary. But whatever they do, and whatever treatment is necessary, you're lucky that this has been found out early. It's not a nice thought but it's better than the alternative. That lovely husband of yours—he spoke to me last night, and he said all he wants is to have you back home safely, no matter what has to be done. He meant it, too. Now, I'm going to give you this injection. Turn over—that's right. Very soon you'll begin to feel pleasantly drowsy. If you want anything, just ring. Here's the bell right beside you.'

While Mrs Loxton was being operated on, Kirsty talked to Sister Dawson. Sister told her that if a mastectomy was found to be necessary, she would make immediate arrangements to have someone who had come through the operation to talk to Mrs Loxton, to reassure her as only someone who had lived through it could do. But when Kirsty went to theatre to bring her patient back, she was told that the biopsy showed that the small lump was benign, and now that it had been removed no further treatment would be necessary.

'Thank you, dearie,' Mrs Loxton murmured drowsily when Kirsty told her this, just before she went off duty. But in case she hadn't really taken it in, Kirsty asked Sister Dawson to mention to night sister that further reassurance might be necessary.

It had been an exhausting day but Kirsty felt, as she went off duty, that she could cope with it now—cope with the demands of a busy city hospital, even on a day like this. She was tired, but it was a good tiredness, a satisfying tiredness.

She was glad, though, that the cheese and wine evening wasn't to take place on theatre day. Glad that she could go back to the flat, have a bath, wash her hair and dress, and by then feel relaxed enough to look forward to the evening.

Mike Wilson was waiting downstairs in the nurses' home and he smiled as she came out of the lift and walked over to him.

'You do look nice, Kirsty,' he said, and she was glad that she had bought the new Indian cotton skirt and the matching blouse in soft greens that she knew did nice things to her eyes. But as she thanked him she couldn't help a small stab of guilt, for she knew very well that it hadn't been Mike Wilson's appreciation she had been thinking of as she dressed, as she brushed her soft brown curls loose on her shoulders.

The big staff canteen was crowded, and as Mike took her hand and drew her through the crowds to the tables at the far end, Kirsty told herself that it was highly unlikely that she would see Adam Brent among so many people. And by the time the evening was half over she had accepted that either he wasn't here, or he was hidden among the crowds.

Mike found seats for them and they sat listening to the speeches, clapping politely at the right times, listening attentively—or fairly attentively, Kirsty had to admit, her eyes still searching—as the visiting Member of Parliament spoke of the hospital's illustrious past and forecast its even more illustrious future.

Then the speeches were over and everyone—doctors, nurses, technicians, therapists—made their way back to the tables. Kirsty, catching a glimpse of her reflection in a glass door, couldn't help thinking wistfully that she would so much have liked Adam Brent to see her like this.

And then she saw him, just a short distance away. He hadn't seen her, but surely he would any moment, Kirsty thought. And in spite of all that she had told herself, all that she had decided, her heart turned over at the thought of Adam Brent looking down at her and seeing her as someone more than just the earnest young nurse he had known in Invertorridon.

'This table's nearer,' she said breathlessly to Mike Wilson, and without waiting for him to follow her, she began to make her way to the table near where Adam Brent was standing.

But it was only when she had almost reached him that she saw the girl beside him. She was tall—taller than Kirsty, although beside Adam she didn't look very tall. Her hair was blonde, a smooth, silken cap on her head, and the cream silk dress she was wearing showed the perfection of her slim figure. By now Kirsty was near enough to see that there was a diamond ring on her left hand—the hand that lay lightly, possessively on Adam Brent's arm.

CHAPTER FOUR

IT WAS too late to turn back, for Adam had seen her.

'Kirsty!' he said, obviously pleased, and he turned to the girl with him.

'This is our new little Scottish staff nurse, Helen, the one I was telling you about. Kirsty, I'd like you to meet my fiancée, Helen Conway. *Sister* Conway when you meet professionally, of course! Helen—Kirsty Macrae.'

Helen Conway's blue eyes—such a deep blue that they were almost violet—studied Kirsty coolly for a moment before she murmured a greeting. All Kirsty wanted was to get away, but Adam was telling Helen about the glen and how much he had enjoyed his short time there.

And then, suddenly, he stopped and looked over Kirsty's head at Mike Wilson.

'Wilson?' Adam said, obviously surprised. 'Did you want something?'

'Only Kirsty, when she's ready,' Mike said cheerfully. 'We're hoping to find some food left.'

Adam Brent looked down at Kirsty and all the warmth had gone from his dark eyes.

'We mustn't hold you up,' he said politely, formally. 'I didn't realise you were with Dr Wilson.'

Kirsty, her throat tight and aching, managed to murmur something before she turned away, with Mike's arm keeping her close to him in the crowded room. She wondered if he also heard Helen Conway's voice, light and amused, as she murmured to Adam—'And you said she'd only just got here? She obviously doesn't believe in wasting time if she's found our Mike already!'

If Mike had heard he gave no sign and they made their way towards the nearest table, now empty.

'Too late,' Mike said regretfully. 'Should we try over at the other side?'

'No,' Kirsty replied quickly. 'I—I could really do with some fresh air, Mike.'

She caught a glimpse of her reflection in the glass door as they went out of the big hall. Her soft green skirt swirled around her legs and she remembered, with a stab, how she had felt as she dressed, brushing her hair loose, hoping her freckles didn't show, seeing how the green of her blouse changed her grey eyes to the same green. And longing, longing, for Adam Brent to see her like this—really see her.

And I don't think he even noticed that I looked any different, she thought bleakly. 'But why should he, and him with a beautiful girl like that wearing his ring?

'I don't think our Adam likes me very much,' Mike commented as they walked along the corridor.

'I didn't think you knew him,' Kirsty said, and she hoped that her voice was steady and cool.

'I didn't until recently,' Mike replied as cheerfully as always. 'But I'm afraid I've crossed his path a couple of times in a rather unfortunate way. Not work-wise, but, er, socially.' He stopped and looked down at her.

'But never mind what Adam Brent thinks of me—I'm much more interested in what Kirsty Macrae thinks of me. Have I told you that I like your hair loose like that? It's much better than pinned under your cap.'

'At least three times,' Kirsty told him. And all at once it helped that Mike was looking down at her with teasing laughter in his eyes. It took away some of the hurt and the shock she had felt when she discovered that Adam Brent was engaged. Determinedly, she pushed away all thoughts of him and smiled up at Mike, who obviously took this as an invitation. His arms held her close to him and his lips were warm on hers, and Kirsty, knowing all too well that she was responding for all the wrong reasons, clung to him.

There had been no one else in the corridor when they stopped, and Kirsty was the first to hear footsteps coming towards them. She drew back from Mike and found herself facing Adam Brent— an Adam looking completely different. His lean, dark face was tight and forbidding and his eyes were cold.

'I'm sorry,' he said brusquely. 'I came after you to ask you to join us—Dr Brown has just organised a tray of sausage rolls—but I see you'd obviously much rather be alone.'

Without another word, he turned and walked back into the hall.

'Sorry about that, Kirsty,' Mike said, not sounding in the least sorry. 'But he's right—we would rather be alone, wouldn't we?'

But the moment when she had found herself responding to Mike had gone—gone in the cool scorn of Adam Brent's eyes resting on her.

'I'm sorry, Mike,' Kirsty murmured, 'but I'd like to go home.'

She was grateful to him for his immediate acceptance of that, grateful that he didn't try to persuade her to change her mind. But as she sat in her room in the little flat in the nurses' home, Kirsty thought bleakly that she had meant exactly what she had said when she told Mike that she wanted to go home. Only it was her home in Scotland she meant, not her room here. With all her heart she longed for the peace of the glens she loved and missed so much.

But Kirsty had never been one for letting things get her down and she kept reminding herself, over the next few days, that the most important thing in her life was that she was a nurse. She told herself firmly that she had been very foolish indeed to have let herself think that she could ever mean anything to Adam Brent. Even without the lovely girl he was engaged to, she was a very new staff nurse and Adam was a surgical registrar. He had been very kind to her in the glen, but she should never have built anything more on it than a passing interest.

Because of him she was here at Luke's to further her training, and that she would do. She would work hard, she would learn all that she could, and then she could go back to the glen and forget all about Adam Brent.

Harding ward was very busy, and Kirsty was glad of that. Sometimes, as she moved swiftly about the ward, as she helped to set up a drip, or removed sutures, adjusted drains, checked on dressings, filled in patients' charts, checked on the special diets that were so important, she found herself thinking that she had never really known what hard work was in the small hospital on the hill. After the first few weeks sister Dawson began to give her more and more responsibility, and Kirsty appreciated this. The older woman would stand by and allow Kirsty to adjust a difficult drip as if she had all the time in the world, and as if she was completely certain that Kirsty would do the job as it should be done. And gradually Kirsty's own confidence increased and she found that she was enjoying the work of the busy ward more and more.

Except when Adam Brent was one of the doctors doing a round. Somehow, then, she found it difficult to keep her mind entirely on what she was doing. It was difficult to remain nothing but a busy and professional young nurse when she was so conscious that, apart from a cool nod, he was ignoring her completely.

Sometimes she was called on to assist Sister Dawson when a dressing had to be removed for

Adam or one of the other doctors to examine, and she would have to concentrate fiercely on keeping her hands steady.

'Careful, Nurse,' Adam said once, quite sharply, as Kirsty removed the dressing so that he could check on his ulcer patient. 'There's no hurry—do it gently.'

'Yes, Dr Brent. Sorry, Dr Brent,' Kirsty murmured in the approved manner as she completed what she had to do.

And afterwards, when Adam had gone, she stood in the sluice where she had taken the dirty dressings and blinked back the tears that were so treacherously close. With the other doctors she was as professional and as efficient as she knew she could and should be. As she was with the patients. It was only when Adam was near that she knew she went to pieces.

She could have coped with a professional distance between them, for that was only what she would expect. And she could cope, too, with the knowledge that he was engaged to Helen Conway, for she had managed to come to terms with that. But she couldn't forget the way he had looked at her when he found her in Mike's arms. She couldn't forget the cool scorn in his voice and in his eyes. It was only a kiss, she reminded herself reasonably more than once, but it was all too obvious that Adam Brent's opinion of her had dropped very sharply indeed.

Slowly, as the days passed, Kirsty knew that she couldn't leave it like this. Somehow she had to make Adam see that—that she wasn't the kind of girl he obviously thought she was.

But that wasn't going to be easy. The only time she saw him was on the ward, or occasionally in the busy and crowded canteen. And she knew very well that she couldn't just walk up to him and start trying to explain. She tried to tell herself that it didn't matter, that if Adam Brent could change his opinion and withdraw his friendship as easily as that, he wasn't worth her bothering about.

But she couldn't forget, ever, what there had been between them in those weeks in the glen, little as it was. All she wanted was the chance to clear the air between them, the chance to make him realise that she was the same Kirsty, that she wasn't cheap, or fast, or any of the things he obviously thought that she was.

Then, just when she had given up all hope of the chance to do this, she met him quite unexpectedly one day in the park. She had come off duty at seven and although it was almost dusk she had walked across to the park, her cloak wrapped tightly around her to shut out the evening chill. Sometimes she needed this short time alone, between the busy ward and the nurses' home, this time of peace and seclusion.

He came round the corner, walking quickly—so quickly that he almost bumped into her. 'Sorry, Nurse,' he said, obviously far away. And then, recognising her, 'Oh, sorry.'

Kirsty didn't give herself time to think, time to wonder if she was doing the right thing.

'Adam,' she said, unsteadily. 'I—I've been wanting to talk to you, to—explain.'

He looked down at her, his face unyielding.

'I don't think there is anything to explain,' he
said, dismissively. 'I presume you're referring to
my interruption of your tender love scene with
young Wilson.' He shrugged. 'Not that it matters in
the slightest to me, but I didn't think you were a girl
like that, Kirsty.'

And now there was something else beside the
hurt—Kirsty could feel the beginning of a slow,
rising anger.

'A girl like what?' she asked him.

'A girl to fall for the sort of fellow young Wilson
is,' Adam replied. 'I don't know whether he told
you, but he's been up before the hospital disciplinary committee, because—'

Kirsty's chin rose. 'I don't want to be told any
tales about Mike,' she said. 'All I know about
the—the sort of fellow he is, is that he's been
friendly and kind and he's helped me to feel at
home here.'

And that is considerably more than you have
done, Dr Adam Brent, she said silently, ignoring
her earlier acceptance of the fact that she had no
right to expect him to give her any special treatment, that she had misinterpreted the friendship
they had had in the glen.

'You'll get yourself talked about if you go around
with Wilson,' Adam said then, abruptly. 'I don't
like to see you getting yourself that kind of a
reputation, Kirsty.'

It was only slight, but the unexpected softening in his voice was almost too much for her.

'Thank you,' she said. 'But I'm capable of looking after myself.' And, because it had all gone so wrong, this chance to put things right with Adam and to clear the air, because she was close to tears and she was determined not to give him the satisfaction of seeing how upset she was, she laughed. 'For goodness' sake, it was just a kiss!'

Adam Brent looked down at her, his face expressionless. And all at once Kirsty was afraid, for there was something very strange in the darkness of his eyes.

'In that case,' he said evenly, 'since kisses mean so little to you—'

Before she could do anything to stop him, he took her in his arms and kissed her, his lips hard and demanding on hers, his arms holding her close to him. Kirsty's small hands beat against his chest, but she was helpless. And in spite of her anger at this man, in spite of the arrogance of the way he was kissing her, there was an immediate tide of response through her whole body.

Abruptly, he let her go.

'I'm sorry,' he said shakily. 'I had no right to do that, it was unforgivable.'

Kirsty's lips felt bruised and she had almost fallen when he released her so suddenly. Somehow, she managed to keep her head high and her voice steady.

'It—doesn't matter,' she said carefully. 'As I said before, it was just a kiss.'

Adam Brent's eyes darkened.

'As you say,' he agreed tightly, 'just a kiss.' And without another word, he turned and left her, walking away into the gathering dusk.

Slowly, Kirsty bent, picked her white cap up from the path and put it back on her head before she turned and walked across the park towards the hospital. She thought that perhaps she was walking like an old woman, or like someone who has been very ill, for she had to concentrate on what she was doing.

What had gone wrong? she wondered, sad and bewildered. She had thought that she could put things right by talking to Adam, by trying to make him see that she was the same Kirsty he had known in Invertorridon. But somehow his opinion of her was even worse, for he thought that she gave her kisses lightly and thoughtlessly.

And I don't, Kirsty told herself, knowing that this was true. Inside her warm cloak, Kirsty shivered. All those months ago in Invertorridon she had thought of Adam kissing her, she had longed for him to kiss her. And now he had. A kiss with no tenderness, no love in it. A kiss that left her feeling cheapened and degraded because that was how he looked on her.

But at the same time she knew that it was going to be very hard to forget her instinctive and immediate response to Adam Brent's kiss. And it was going to be far from easy to see him in the hospital, to work beside him, and to behave as if nothing had happened between them.

CHAPTER FIVE

KIRSTY knew all too well that she would have found the next few weeks even more difficult without Mike Wilson's friendship.

He was always fun to be with, light-hearted and cheerful, and, a little to Kirsty's surprise, undemanding and obviously prepared to stick to the rules and the limits she had set. And gradually, as she began to know him better, Kirsty realised that under the laughter there was an interest and a commitment to his work that was somehow unexpected.

Jane Farrant, Kirsty's flatmate, was unable to hide her surprise at the friendship between Kirsty and Mike.

'Friendship?' she said one day when Kirsty used the word. 'Kirsty, you're a dear sweet innocent! I've known Mike for a few years and I don't think I've ever known him to have a relationship with a girl which could be described as friendship.'

'Well, *this* is,' Kirsty told her, with certainty.

Jane leaned forward. 'You know, of course,' she said, for once serious, 'that Mike's been up before the committee a couple of times recently?'

'Yes, I know,' Kirsty replied steadily, and she remembered Adam Brent telling her this. 'At least, I mean I know he has, but I don't know why, and—I don't think it really matters.'

Jane looked at her thoughtfully. 'No, but all the same you should know about it. Oh, I'm not telling tales—everyone knows. The first time, Mike was found in one of the second floor rooms right here in the nurses' home when we had an unexpected fire drill.'

'Och, well,' Kirsty said, a little surprised, 'I'm sure he wouldn't be the first young doctor to do that!'

Jane's clear blue eyes were amused.

'They weren't playing tiddly-winks, you know,' she said. 'And it was three o'clock in the morning.'

To her annoyance, Kirsty felt a flood of colour stain her cheeks.

'I don't think I want to hear any—' she began.

'And the other time,' Jane went on, 'he kept one of the second-year girls out all night. When he brought her back he tried to reverse his car against the wall so that she could climb up on it and get in the window, and he reversed into a dustbin. And, of course, they were caught, questions were asked, the answers weren't very satisfactory—and there he was, back before the committee. It didn't seem to bother him too much, I must say.'

But it did bother Adam, Kirsty thought, and somewhat unwillingly she had to admit to herself that perhaps Adam had had some reason to feel that she wouldn't do her reputation any good by being seen around with Mike. Now that she had heard this, she could understand why Adam hadn't been too happy to see that she was with Mike that night of the cheese and wine party. And what he had seen when he came along the corridor and found her in Mike's arms, must have, in a way, confirmed his feelings. Reluctantly, but inevitably, because she was a fairminded girl, Kirsty had to admit that she could understand that.

But what she couldn't understand, and couldn't justify, was the way he had behaved when she had tried to talk to him in the park. He hadn't given her a chance. His mind had been made up. He had been quite certain that he knew what sort of a girl Kirsty was and he had treated her accordingly. All right, he had apologised, he had said it was unforgivable. And it was, Kirsty told herself defiantly. And him a man engaged to be married, too. He had no right to treat me like that, no right at all.

And in any case, she thought sometimes—for although she had made up her mind that she would waste no more thinking on Adam Brent, she found that this was easier said than done and there were many times when she re-lived those few moments in the park—in any case, surely Adam, having known her in the glen, even for such a short time, might have been more ready to accept that she wasn't the same as some of the other girlfriends Mike had had.

Somehow, that was the thing that made Kirsty saddest of all. Those few weeks when they had known each other in Invertorridon, those weeks that had meant everything in the world to her, had obviously been of so little importance to Adam that he couldn't even weigh the Kirsty he had known then against the girl he now thought her to be.

It would have been easier, she often felt, if she had been working on another ward and coming into less contact with Adam. But since he was junior surgical registrar and Harding was one of the surgical wards, it was inevitable that he was in and out fairly often.

And no matter what she might feel about him personally, Kirsty knew that Adam Brent was a good doctor. A promising young surgeon, she heard Sister Dawson say more than once when they talked about the doctors.

'Have you ever seen him operate?' Kirsty once asked, unable to keep herself from showing the interest she felt, although she would like to have felt more detached.

Sister Dawson shook her head.

'I don't need to,' she returned. 'Almost every day we're dealing with cases Adam Brent has operated on. Have you ever seen a bad cut, or an infected wound, or a clumsy suture job come up from the theatre with Adam Brent's name on it? No, neither have I. And what's more, there aren't many doctors more conscientious than he is in their post-operative care.' She shook her head. 'Such a waste, him engaged to that girl.'

'A waste?' Kirsty said, unable to hide her surprise. 'But she's a lovely girl. And she's a sister here, isn't she?'

'Oh, she's lovely all right,' the older woman agreed. 'And yes, she's a sister here, over in

Daniels—that's womens' medical. But there are sisters and sisters. And Helen Conway just isn't one of my favourite people.'

She stood up and straightened her apron. 'But what am I doing, sitting here gossiping when we have the medicines to do! Here's the drug cupboard key, Nurse Macrae, and the list—take young Andrea with you and bring me back the list and the key when you're ready.'

Kirsty did as she was told and went along to the drug cupboard with Andrea Johnson, for one of the rules that no nurse would dream of breaking was that *two* nurses went together to the drug cupboard. No one ever dealt with the drugs and medicines alone.

After the medicine round she had to check that her juniors had done the blood pressure round and the careful monitoring of intake and output of fluids, and then it was time to supervise tea while Sister Dawson was off to have her own break.

It was the day before theatre day and there were, as always, a number of patients now admitted and being prepared for early operations. Kirsty took some tea to the patient in the end bed in the big ward, and it was only as she set the tray down on the bed-table that she saw that the young woman's eyes were red. Kirsty hesitated, but only for a moment. There was a great deal to do but nothing so urgent that she couldn't spare a few moments to find out what was troubling young Mrs Miller.

'Have a cup of tea, Mrs Miller,' she said quietly. She hesitated and then told her patient again what would happen the following morning. 'You're lucky, you're scheduled early, so you won't even be bothered by seeing the others having breakfast—you'll be pretty drowsy by that time. The night staff will give you your pre-med and after that you can't get out of bed because you'll be fairly drowsy very quickly, so you're to ring if you want anything at all.' She smiled, hoping she sounded reassuring. 'Unfortunately, as I'm sure you know, you won't even be allowed to have a cup of tea at that stage, but I don't think you'll be worrying. One lady last week told us she felt as if she just floated down to the theatre!'

There was no answering smile from the girl in the bed.

'Is it the operation itself that's worrying you, Mrs Miller?' Kirsty asked gently. 'I know you're young to be having a hysterectomy, but with this history of fibroids I'm sure you'll feel so much better once it's done. You've been pretty ill, I see, and you must have been tired most of the time. This really will make the world of difference to you.'

Young Mrs Miller's grey eyes met Kirsty's. 'I know that,' she said quietly. 'My doctor has explained it all and I know it has to be done. But it's the end of all my hopes for a family, Nurse. I've had three miscarriages and I know I wouldn't be able to carry a baby full-term, but there was always the faint hope that maybe next time it would be all right. Now, well, after this, that's it. No more hope at all.'

Kirsty had never been able to achieve the detachment that many nurses did, and now her eyes filled with tears.

'I am sorry,' she said. 'I didn't realise that. No wonder you're feeling pretty low.' She waited while Mrs Miller drank some of her tea. 'How does your husband feel?' she asked.

Now the young woman managed to smile. 'He's more worried about me than about the prospect of babies,' she said. 'Oh, he's disappointed—don't get me wrong, Nurse, he would make a marvellous father, but—I suppose it's easier for him to face up to it than for me. He thinks we should put our names down to adopt, but I don't know. It wouldn't be the same.'

Unobtrusively, Kirsty refilled the teacup and pushed it a little nearer.

'I don't think you should even think about it until you get over this operation,' she said then, firmly. 'You get this over and get back on your feet, and then see how you feel. But don't close your mind to adoption—I have a cousin who has two little adopted boys and now one of her own, and she says that really and truly she feels the same for all three. And the funny thing is, the little adopted boys actually look more like their parents than their own child does!'

'I've heard that does happen,' Mrs Miller agreed. And then she looked over Kirsty's shoulder. 'Oh, Dr Brent! I didn't think I'd see you until tomorrow.'

Kirsty, her face unaccountably colouring, turned round to find Adam Brent standing there.

'Oh—I'm sorry, Dr Brent, I didn't hear you coming,' she murmured, confused. Adam Brent only nodded to her.

'I just thought I'd look in and see how you were feeling, Mrs Miller,' he said to his patient. 'I'm only assisting, of course, but I'll be there to say hello to you before you go to sleep tomorrow. Right, let's have a look at you.'

Kirsty drew the screens around the bed and then Sister Dawson came to join Adam, so she was able to retreat to the duty room, wondering, as she wrote up the reports on the Kardex files, just how long he had been standing there. Standing there, listening to me talking all that rubbish about my cousin she thought, annoyed at herself for not having seen Adam coming.

She concentrated fiercely on what she was doing—so fiercely that once again she didn't hear Adam Brent until he coughed.

'Nurse Macrae,' he said stiffly. It was the first time he had spoken directly to her since he had walked away from her that evening in the park. There had been many times on the ward when they had been together with a patient, but this was the first time he had addressed her by name.

'Yes, Dr Brent?' Kirsty replied, and she hoped that her voice was steady.

'Thank you for talking to Mrs Miller the way you did,' he said unexpectedly. 'She's been feeling pretty low. Somehow you found the right thing to say and the right way to say it.' He hesitated, but Kirsty didn't say anything and he went on, a little awkwardly, 'I just wanted to mention it and to thank you, that's all.'

And of course that's all, Kirsty told herself sensibly as Adam Brent walked away along the corridor. He is a good doctor and he appreciates good nursing. But it was nice of him to take the trouble to mention it to me, considering that he can't have found it easy to be speaking to me at all. Nor me to him.

And there was a pang, then, for the long and easy conversations the two of them had had last summer in the glen, the way they had been able to share their thoughts and their feelings about the work that meant so much to both of them. But where was the good, Kirsty asked herself briskly, in thinking like that? Brooding about the past in this unhealthy way was far from sensible, and she had always prided herself on being a sensible girl. And I'll go on being one, she told herself firmly.

And so the sensible girl refused to let herself admit how much it had meant to her that Adam Brent had appreciated the way she had talked to Mrs Miller. And that night the same sensible girl accepted Mike Wilson's invitation to a party, although on the way there she did express her doubts to him.

'It's not to be one of your wild parties, now is it, Mike?' she asked him.

'Cross my heart and hope to die,' he promised her solemnly, with only a twitch of his mouth to tell her of the laughter that was near. And then, with a glance and with teasing in his voice, 'And just what have you been hearing about my wild parties, Kirsty Macrae?'

'Not a great deal,' Kirsty told him honestly. 'But I have heard that you and some of the other young doctors have got quite a reputation for parties that are maybe—well, maybe a wee bit livelier than they might be?'

Mike threw back his head and laughed. 'Kirsty, I love you,' he told her. 'I've never met a girl like you before. Yes, I admit I have been to a few parties that you could probably describe as lively—and I'll admit at the same time that we were all mighty lucky that none of the disciplinary committee got to hear about them.' He put his arm around her and hugged her.

'But surely you know I'm a changed character now?' he asked her. 'Since I met you the old wild Mike has gone and this is a new me.'

Kirsty giggled. 'Och, away with you, Mike,' she told him. 'You'll not have me believing that a leopard like you can change his spots!'

'I'm telling you, Kirsty, I'm completely re-formed, thanks to you,' Mike protested. But he was smiling and Kirsty smiled too at the thought of him changing at all. For wasn't this a nice friendship they had, the two of them, she thought contentedly.

They would go out together maybe a couple of times a week, and Mike would always bring her back to the nurses' home at the right time and kiss her goodnight—and she had to admit it was very pleasant being kissed goodnight by Mike, with him so good-looking and such fun, too.

And she'd had no trouble at all with him once she had told him how she felt. Yes, it was a nice friendship—and perhaps Adam Brent would be a little surprised at it. Perhaps he might find it hard to believe, but that was the way of it. A pleasant friendship, with no strings attached. Just what we both want, Kirsty often told herself.

Soon after that Kirsty had to do a month's night duty. Because the whole hospital was so short-staffed, most of the time she was in charge of Harding ward. At first she felt the responsibility very heavily, not having Sister Dawson there for support, but already the time she had spent here at St Luke's had given her confidence and before long she was reasonably relaxed about feeling that she could cope with any emergency that might arise. There were always doctors on call and she had juniors. And night sister was on the floor below, available if she was needed.

One night when Kirsty took over there was a new patient in the small side ward and screens around the bed.

'Motorcycle accident,' Sister Dawson told her. 'Fractured femur, badly concussed, internal damage. Adam Brent operated but her condition is far from stabilised. We can't special, but Dr Brent wants hourly checks and you're to call him if there's any change.'

When the day staff had gone and Kirsty did her ward round, she was shocked to see how young the girl in the side ward was. Seventeen—and she might not live. Carefully, conscientiously, Kirsty charted the girl's progress and then went on with her other work, fitting in the hourly checks on the girl's condition as Adam Brent had requested.

It was just after midnight when she went quietly back into the small ward and found Adam Brent there.

'Thanks, Nurse,' he said, without looking round, hearing her come in. 'Her condition is unchanged, I see. Not that I expected much, but—oh, I didn't know you were on night duty,' he said flatly.

'Do you want me to do anything, Dr Brent?' Kirsty asked as composedly as she could. He shook his head.

'I just wanted to check for myself. I'll sit here for a bit.'

Half an hour later he was still there. Kirsty stood at the door, and in the moment before he saw her, she realised how weary he was. If she had thought about her next move she wouldn't have done it, because of how things were between them. But she didn't give herself time to think.

'I've just made coffee, Dr Brent,' she said, her voice low. 'Would you like some?'

He hesitated, but only for a moment.

'I would, thank you,' he said, a little awkwardly. 'No, I'll come along to the duty room.'

Both her juniors were working in the sluice and Kirsty poured two mugs of coffee and handed one to Adam Brent, sitting in the chair at the desk. Kirsty sat silent, unsure what to say or to do.

'The boy she was with was killed,' Adam Brent

said after a moment, as if they were in the middle of a conversation. 'He didn't even make it as far as the hospital, and until we can assess any brain damage, I find myself wondering if it might have been better for this child here if she hadn't made it either. And also unncessary. A little more care, a little less speed—' He looked at her, but Kirsty wondered if he really saw her. 'I'm sorry, this is one of the things that catches me every time. I've just spoken to the boy's parents. I might have to speak to hers too, before long.'

'If she does live,' Kirsty said slowly, 'and if she's all right, surely she'll have learned something worth learning?'

Adam thought about that.

'Yes, she probably will,' he agreed. 'But next week, or the week after, there will be another accident, another boy or girl brought in to us in a state like this one. And what can we do?'

He looked at her as if he really expected her to have an answer.

'Just go on patching them up, I suppose,' Kirsty said at last, hesitantly. 'It's our job. Sometimes it works, sometimes it doesn't.'

Adam's dark eyes lightened just a little.

'You win some, you lose some?' he suggested.

'I suppose so,' Kirsty said doubtfully. 'And you try to think mostly about those you win.' He sat up straighter.

'Kirsty,' he began, uncertainly. 'I—'

But she never knew what he meant to say, for at that moment Mike Wilson came along the corridor, his white coat open, his stethoscope slung around his neck.

'Ah, the angel of mercy dispensing coffee, I see,' he said cheerfully. 'So I've come at the right time.'

Adam Brent turned round and Kirsty realised that Mike hadn't known who the doctor was, for it wasn't uncommon for a doctor doing a late round to be given a cup of coffee.

'Are you here to see a patient, Dr Wilson?' Adam Brent asked, and Mike coloured.

'Well—not exactly,' he replied.

Adam Brent stood up. 'I would suggest, Dr Wilson, that you try to keep your professional life and your social life separate.'

At the door, he turned. 'And I would suggest you do the same, Nurse Macrae.'

CHAPTER SIX

'KIRSTY, I'm sorry,' Mike said soberly. 'I just thought I'd look in and see you—cheer you up in your lonely vigil, sort of. But I never thought of Adam Brent being here.'

'It doesn't matter, Mike,' Kirsty said, knowing all too well that it did. She couldn't really be angry with Mike—it was always difficult to be angry with him, she found. But if only he hadn't come—if only Adam had been able to go on and say whatever he had been going to say.

At the same time, she couldn't help thinking that Adam Brent was all too quick to jump to conclusions—and not always the right conclusions—where she was concerned. He had behaved as if she had set up the meeting with Mike, taking advantage of being on night duty, of being alone on the ward. Although, Kirsty admitted to herself with considerable reluctance, that was certainly how it must have looked.

'I don't suppose I'm getting any coffee now,' Mike said meekly.

'Och well, now that you're here I suppose I could give you a cup,' Kirsty replied, smiling in spite of herself at the unaccustomed and barely credible humility of the young doctor. She poured some coffee for him, and when she had given it to him she said seriously, 'But Mike, you really mustn't do this again. Dr Brent was quite right, really. It—it isn't right, you coming here to see me when I'm working.'

Mike put his cup down and took both her hands in his.

'I really am sorry, Kirsty,' he told her earnestly. Then he put one hand over his heart. 'But now that you're on night duty, I hardly ever see you. You're either working or sleeping. I had to come!'

Kirsty shook her head. 'It's a good thing it's a doctor you are, Mike, and not an actor, for you'd ham anything,' she told him, smiling. 'Get away with you, and your stories of having to come. There are plenty other girls just waiting for you to take them out. And hurry up and finish your coffee, now, for night sister will be here soon.'

'I don't want any other girls, just you,' Mike protested. 'And night sister is a pal of mine, she wouldn't be so hard-hearted!'

'Hard-hearted or not, finish your coffee and go,' Kirsty told him.

He sighed, but did what he was told. And just in time, too, Kirsty thought five minutes later, when night sister did appear for her round.

'Everything quiet here with you, Nurse Macrae?' she asked.

'Yes, Sister, thank you,' Kirsty replied, telling herself that one very angry registrar and one supposedly heart-broken intern didn't really count, since all the patients were quiet. By the time Kirsty went off duty in the morning, Adam's patient was

still in much the same condition, although by
evening she seemed to be in a less deep level of
unconsciousness.

'Dr Brent wants to be called if there is any
change,' Sister Dawson told Kirsty. 'Meanwhile,
the same routine—hourly checks. And he really
does mean *any* change—he wants to have some
idea of possible brain damage as soon as possible.'

Throughout the night Kirsty checked Adam's
patient carefully, but there was no change and
when she went off duty the following morning she
couldn't help remembering that Adam had said
that if there was brain damage, it might have been
better if the girl hadn't lived.

Once again, the next night, Sister Dawson told
her there had been no change, and Kirsty was
prepared for this situation to go on. But just after
midnight one of her juniors came to her.

'Nurse Macrae,' she said breathlessly, 'the accident girl—I'm sure her eyes flickered just now!'

Kirsty put down the charts she had been filling in
and walked along to the small side ward. She stood
with the junior at the side of the bed where the girl
lay, still and silent. And then, just as she was about
to tell the younger nurse to stay and to call her if
anything happened, the girl's eyes opened. For a
moment, she looked right into Kirsty's face, and
then she sighed and closed her eyes again.

'Stay with her, Nurse,' Kirsty said quietly. 'I'm
going to call Dr Brent.'

She went back to the duty room and called the
number Adam had left. It was a moment or two

before he answered and his voice was blurred with sleep.

'Yes? Adam Brent here.'

'Dr Brent, this is Nurse Macrae,' Kirsty said quickly, professionally. 'Your patient in Harding has just opened her eyes. Briefly, but she did open them.'

Now Adam's voice was as professional as hers.

'Thank you, Nurse,' he said briskly. 'I'll be right along.'

It took him less than five minutes and Kirsty couldn't help noticing, with an unexpected lurch of her heart, that his dark hair was still rumpled. She went with him along the corridor and stood by while he examined the patient.

'Julie?' he said clearly. 'Julie, open your eyes.'

Kirsty felt that she had been holding her breath for hours, as she waited. At last the eyelids flickered again and the girl on the bed opened her eyes.

'Julie, I'm Dr Brent,' Adam said quietly. 'You know you've been in an accident?' The bandaged head moved fractionally.

'Road—wet,' she murmured, her voice such a thin thread that both Kirsty and Adam had to lean closer to hear her. 'The bike slipped.' And then her eyes opened wide and she murmured, urgently, '*Peter?*'

Kirsty was so close to Adam that she could feel him stiffen, feel him catch his breath. But only for a moment, and then he said steadily, 'I'm sorry, Julie. Peter is dead.'

'I—think I knew that,' the girl whispered with an effort. She turned her head to the side, but not before Kirsty had seen the tears that filled her eyes. The movement brought a small gasp of pain, and Adam said quietly that he was going to give her an injection to relieve it and to let her sleep. He stood beside the bed, looking down at the girl until the injection began to take effect and she fell into a sleep that, although it was drug-induced, was more natural than her previous state.

'She'll do, I think,' he said tiredly as he went out of the room, followed by Kirsty. 'We'll run some tests on her tomorrow, but she can talk rationally. I think she'll be all right.' He stopped and looked down at Kirsty, and she thought that for this moment he had forgotten the way they had parted two nights ago when Mike had come. 'I'm sorry I had to do that—tell her about her boyfriend. But I've come to the conclusion that there is never a right time for bad news. If I hadn't told her she would have worried and, sooner or later, she would have had to be told.'

'I think you were right,' she said quietly. 'She probably had some memory of the accident and just after it, and if you hadn't told her she would have gone over and over the whole thing in her mind. Now she knows and she has to begin accepting it, hard as it is.'

Adam nodded. But she saw that his jaw had tightened and his dark eyes were once again cool and remote.

'Thanks for calling me, Nurse,' he said, and he

turned and walked away down the corridor.

And just what did I expect? Kirsty asked herself reasonably. Do I not know well enough the opinion Dr Brent has of me? But there was an ache and a tightness in her throat that would not be dispelled. Thank goodness I have three nights off now, and I can have something of a normal life again, Kirsty thought. I'm tired, that's mostly what's wrong with me.

And she *was* tired. When she went off duty the next morning she went straight to bed, slept through the rest of that day, got up to have something to eat in the evening, then went back to bed and slept right through the night. The next morning she felt human again. She went for a walk in the park in the morning and in the afternoon she went shopping with Jane, who had a few hours off duty.

'Now we'll have a cup of real coffee,' Jane said at about four, and they went into a little coffee-shop that she knew. 'Real coffee and some nice, fattening cakes. Just as well neither you nor I need to worry about that!'

When they had almost finished, she looked at Kirsty curiously.

'And now, Kirsty,' she said firmly, 'I'd like to know just what you've done to Mike.'

'What I've done to Mike?' Kirsty replied, surprised.

Jane waved one hand. 'Don't pretend you don't know what I mean,' she said. 'I've known Mike a long time—he and I had quite a thing at one time, but it didn't last because we both wanted to be free. But Mike has changed, Kirsty. He was at the party I was at a couple of nights ago, and he enjoyed it, he had fun, but he acted as if something was missing. And I think that something was you.'

'Mike and I are just—' Kirsty began, defensively.

'I know, I know,' Jane said airily. 'You're just good friends. Sure, I believe that's how you see it, Kirsty, but I'm not so sure about Mike. Do you know what I think?'

Kirsty didn't want to know what Jane thought, because she was beginning to have all too good an idea, but there was no stopping her friend.

'I think that Mike is in love with you,' Jane said. 'Or well on the way to being in love with you.'

Kirsty stirred her coffee, unwilling to meet Jane's questioning eyes.

'I'm sure you're wrong,' she said, but she knew that there was uncertainty in her voice. Because she couldn't help remembering, now that Jane had said this, some of the things Mike had said. Oh, she had treated them lightly and he had let it go, but she had had a slightly uneasy feeling at the time, a feeling she had managed to dismiss. And not only some of the things he had said but the way he looked at her sometimes, with all the laughter gone from his blue eyes, as if—as if he was waiting. And I can't let him be waiting for me, Kirsty thought forlornly, for Mike's friendship had come to mean a great deal to her.

Her chin rose. 'I'm sure you're wrong, Jane,' she said again. 'But—but maybe I should just be having a word with Mike, to make sure that he isn't getting any wrong ideas.'

'And why should you do that?' Jane asked curiously. 'I can tell you, Kirsty, there are plenty of nurses here at Luke's who'd give their eye-teeth to have Mike Wilson falling in love with them— and reforming at the same time!' Kirsty felt her cheeks grow warm.

'I don't want Mike to be in love with me,' she murmured, distressed. 'His friendship means a great deal to me, but I couldn't be letting him think that it was anything more than that.'

Jane put her cup down. 'Why not?' she asked. 'Is there someone else, Kirsty? You haven't mentioned anyone.'

'No, there isn't anyone,' Kirsty said quickly— perhaps too quickly, she thought. But it was true. There wasn't anyone else. 'It's just—I don't feel that way about Mike.'

'Give yourself time, my girl,' Jane advised. 'Don't go burning your bridges. Mike Wilson has always been great fun and I have a feeling that this new Mike could still be fun, and be quite something as well.'

They finished their coffee and left then, and Jane said nothing more about Mike and his possible feelings. But Kirsty was uneasy and that night, when she went to a film with Mike, she found that for the first time she was self-conscious with him— watching what she said and, perhaps even more, watching what he said. And the way he said it.

'Relax, Kirsty,' he said once, with such perception that she coloured. 'I'm not going to eat you—or anything else! I know the rules.'

And when he took her back to the nurses' home he kissed her very gently.

'You're tired,' he said softly. 'Go in and go to bed—I'll be glad when you're finished with night duty.'

'Somebody has to do it,' Kirsty pointed out.

'Oh yes,' Mike agreed. 'But not my girl.'

She wanted to say—*I'm not your girl*. But she didn't, because he had said it so lightly and she thought that perhaps both she and Jane had been wrong. It was Mike's way, after all.

'Remember,' he said as she got out of the car, 'you're coming to that party with me on Friday. I know you're off that night because I checked.'

In spite of herself, Kirsty smiled. 'Then I can't very well refuse, can I?' she said.

It was always strange going back on night duty after a few days off, but Kirsty found that here on Harding she was enjoying night duty more than she ever had as a student. Probably because of the extra responsibility, she decided.

Adam's young patient had made considerable progress in the few days that Kirsty was off. Most of the time she was fairly bright, and Sister Dawson told Kirsty that Adam Brent was satisfied that there was no brain damage.

'Her femur and her other injuries will take time, of course,' she said, going over the list of patients with Kirsty. 'But she's a lucky girl.'

I suppose she is, Kirsty thought later, as she

stood at the door of the small ward and watched young Julie for a few moments, unobserved. But I wonder if she thinks that herself at the moment.

'Hello, Julie,' she said gently.

The girl turned round and brushed her hand across her eyes.

'Hello, Nurse Macrae,' she replied. 'I've missed you.'

'You look much better than you did when I went off duty,' Kirsty told her.

'I feel much better,' Julie said. 'Only—' She stopped, and her eyes filled with tears.

'I know,' Kirsty said gently. 'Were you very fond of him, Julie?'

'It wasn't a big deal or anything,' the girl said, unsteadily. 'But we'd been going around together for quite a while and—and he loved that bike, Nurse. It seems so awful that that was what killed him.' She tried to smile. 'Sorry, but sometimes it gets too much for me. Dr Brent says if I feel like crying, I should cry. He's quite a guy, isn't he?'

'Yes, he is,' Kirsty agreed. 'He certainly did a good job on you.'

Now that Julie was so much better, Kirsty hadn't expected Adam to come up to the ward at night, but he had another patient recovering from a gall-bladder removal, and because Kirsty was in charge she had to accompany him to both his patients and stand by while he examined them and talked to them.

In spite of her determination to remain detached and professional as far as Adam was concerned, she watched his hands, strong and brown and reassuring, and she listened to the interest and the sympathy in his voice, and knew that her instinctive feeling about him all those months ago in Invertorridon had been right. This was a good doctor and a good man. And a man who would always be very special to her, no matter what he thought of her.

'Thank you, Nurse,' Adam Brent said as she removed the dressing. For a moment his dark eyes met hers, a moment of shared professional pleasure in the steady recovery of a patient they had worked and cared for together. Then he turned away. But in that moment Kirsty knew, with complete certainty, that these fleeting contacts with Adam Brent meant far more to her than any time she spent with Mike. It had been the truth when she said to Jane that there was no one else, because this was as far as it would go. But because of the way she felt about Adam, she knew that she had to be honest with Mike. Not honest to the extent of telling him how she felt about Adam Brent, but honest to the extent of telling him, as lightly and as kindly as she could, that she looked on their relationship as friendship and nothing more, and she hoped that he did too.

It isn't going to be easy, Kirsty realised, concerned, when she was at the Friday night party with Mike. I certainly can't tell him in the middle of all this.

She hoped with all her heart that she wouldn't lose Mike's friendship, that once she had got the air cleared he would be prepared to go on seeing her, but she knew that she couldn't just let things drift and risk hurting him. But not tonight, she thought, as he whirled her around the crowded floor to an old Beatles' record someone had brought along.

'I haven't any breath left, Mike,' she protested, laughing. 'Let's sit down for a bit.'

All the furniture had been cleared from the room—the flat belonged to two young doctors who worked with Mike—and there were some cushions against the walls. They sat down and Mike managed to find two glasses of wine.

'Here's to us, Kirsty,' he said, touching her glass with his.

'Mike,' she began, troubled, but the room was noisy and it was impossible to have a private conversation, so she left it.

'Hey, I see Helen of Troy is slumming tonight,' Mike said with interest. Kirsty saw Helen Conway, Adam's fiancée, at the other side of the room. Her heart turned over, but there was no sign of Adam's tall figure beside Helen.

'Is she on her own?' she asked carefully. 'I mean—isn't Dr Brent with her?'

'She isn't on her own, but Dr Brent isn't with her,' Mike said, and now Kirsty could see there was a man with Helen—younger, slighter than Adam. 'Steve Hartley being honoured this time, I see.'

'This time?' Kirsty asked, in spite of herself.

'I couldn't honestly say our Adam is one of my favourite people,' Mike said thoughtfully, 'although he's a damned good surgeon. But I don't like to see him being messed around like this. I've heard a few stories about her not being too happy to sit in when he's working. Heck, they've only been engaged a few months, I believe!'

A few months, Kirsty thought. So Adam hadn't been engaged when he was at Invertorridon. For some absurd reason she was pleased at this.

'She certainly seems to be having a good time,' she commented.

Mike turned to her. 'So am I,' he said, softly. 'Just because you're with me—that's all I need, Kirsty.'

Then, his seriousness gone, he pulled her to her feet and started dancing again. But that night as Kirsty was falling asleep, she knew that she had to talk to Mike; she had to make him understand that she wasn't prepared to let him think that she felt anything more than friendship for him. The next time I'm off, she promised herself, I'll talk to him.

But two days later, when she had just come off duty at seven in the morning and fallen into a heavy sleep, she was wakened by a knocking at her door and Jane's voice calling her name.

'Kirsty? Wake up, Kirsty.' Then she was in the room, her hand on Kirsty's shoulder.

'Kirsty, wake up,' she said urgently.

'What's wrong?' Kirsty asked, and now she saw that Jane was very white.

'There's been an accident,' Jane told her. 'It's Mike—he's in intensive care.'

CHAPTER SEVEN

IT WAS a moment before Kirsty could say anything.

'How badly hurt is he?' she asked then, knowing, even as she said it, that it had to be bad because he was in intensive care. Jane shook her head.

'I don't know,' she said unsteadily. 'I'm in out-patients just now, next to casualty, and of course we hear the ambulances and always know when there's been a bad accident. But this time there seemed to be more coming and going. Then one of the juniors heard a doctor mention that it was one of our own men and that he'd been out on an emergency call. I—I asked Sister if I could go and find out and they told me it was Mike.' She stood up.

'I shouldn't be here, of course,' she said. 'But I asked sister if I could come and tell you. I didn't want you to wake up and go to the canteen and hear it there. I'll have to go back now.'

Kirsty looked at her friend. 'I think you'd better have a cup of good, strong tea first,' she told her. 'You're very white, Jane.'

'I've known Mike a long time,' the other girl said slowly, 'and we've always been friends. You'd think we'd be able to take things like this in our stride, wouldn't you, Kirsty? But it's such a shock when it's someone you know.'

She went to the door. 'I'll get some tea later,' she said, with an obvious effort. 'We're pretty busy— I can't leave sister with only juniors. Kirsty, if you hear anything more, come round to outpatients and let me know.'

When Jane had gone Kirsty dressed, pulling on jeans and a jersey, tying her hair back from her face. And all the time shutting out the thought of Mike lying in intensive care, white and still.

The intensive care unit was on the same floor as the theatres but in another wing, a wing that was separate and had restricted entry. Kirsty knew this and she went into the small waiting-room on the landing where she could see anyone going to the unit, or leaving it.

For once there was no one else waiting, and she was grateful for that; grateful that there was no one to see her sitting tensely, her eyes fixed on the door. She never knew how long she sat there but it seemed like a lifetime before a staff nurse came hurrying out. Kirsty didn't know her but she stood up and walked towards her.

'Can you tell me how Mike Wilson is, Nurse?' she asked urgently.

The nurse, who was only a few years older than Kirsty herself, stopped.

'Are you a relative?' she asked.

Kirsty shook her head.

'Just a friend,' she said quietly.

The older nurse smiled—a smile that Kirsty knew was professional, reassuring and meaning-less.

'I'm sorry,' she said. 'I can't really say anything. Dr Brent is with him now and everything possible is being done for him. Perhaps if you come back in a few hours there might be some news.'

Kirsty sat down again. Of course, she told herself, that's all she *could* say. She isn't in a position to give me information and she's not going to give me any false hopes. She thought of the many times she had told relatives that the patient was as well as could be expected. Sometimes she had wished that she could say more, and now she understood even better how *they* felt, being given information that was really no information at all.

There was a drinks machine, so she got herself some tea and sat down on the couch to wait. Everything seemed distant and unreal to her. It just didn't seem possible that two nights ago Mike had kissed her goodnight, his blue eyes warm and teasing, and had said that he would see her soon. And now he was lying there, a patient instead of a doctor, and she didn't know anything about the accident or his condition.

I think, Kirsty decided with careful detachment, that I must be in a state of shock. I don't think I've really taken this in yet.

She had seen, so many times, this reaction in the relatives of people who had been taken ill seriously and unexpectedly. Now, for the first time, she could understand how they felt. None of it seemed to be real. She had a feeling that she would wake up soon, that she would find it had all been nothing but a bad dream.

When she had finished her tea she set her cup down carefully, for she was suddenly realising just how tired she was, having come off night duty. She'd only had half an hour's sleep before Jane came. She leaned her head back and closed her eyes wearily. But she didn't fall asleep, and the moment the door to the intensive care unit opened she sat up quickly.

Adam Brent, closing the door behind him, stopped. Kirsty stood up and went across the room to him.

'How is he?' she asked quietly. 'How badly hurt is he?'

Adam looked down at her, compassion in his dark eyes, so that even before he spoke she knew it was bad.

'He's pretty bad, Kirsty,' he told her quietly. 'We've removed a clot that was causing pressure on his brain and we've set a couple of minor fractures, but we don't dare risk doing anything further yet, until his condition stabilises.'

And suddenly, with his words, the dream-like unreality was gone. It had happened and she wasn't going to wake up. The nightmare was real and the pain of it tore through Kirsty. Mike, her dear, good friend, so badly hurt that the surgeon couldn't yet risk finding out the extent of the damage.

'Steady, Kirsty,' Adam Brent said, and he put his arm around her. 'Sit down. This must have been a dreadful shock to you.'

She nodded, unable to speak for a while.

'How did it happen?' she asked at last, her lips stiff.

'Apparently he was on call and there was an emergency. He set off on his own, and he was to call in if an ambulance was needed. I haven't got all the details, but it seems the accident wasn't his fault at all. Some fool came through a red light and smashed into Dr Wilson's car. He didn't have a chance.'

He didn't have a chance. The words went on and on inside Kirsty's head, bleakly. And then the question she couldn't ask, the question Adam couldn't answer yet. Did he have a chance now?

Adam looked at his watch. 'I'm operating in ten minutes, Kirsty. I have to go,' he said quietly. His eyes rested on her face. 'There really is nothing you can do here—you know that as well as I do. Please go and get some rest and come back later. I believe his parents have been sent for, but it will take them some time to get here. They live in Cornwall.'

Kirsty shook her head. 'I'll stay here,' she said, for she knew that she couldn't go any further away than this little waiting-room. She looked up at Adam. 'I don't suppose I could see him?'

The surgeon shook his head.

'Not at the moment,' he told her decisively. 'But I promise you, Kirsty, that as soon as I feel it's possible, you can see him.'

After all there had been between them, the unexpected kindness in his voice and in his eyes brought a blur of tears to her own eyes.

'You're very kind,' she said, not quite steadily.

For a long time, he looked down at her. 'I'm sorry, Kirsty,' he said at last, and she had the strange certainty that he wasn't only talking about Mike's accident.

She sat down on the couch again to wait, and the leaden minutes and hours slowly went by. At some time she leaned her head back and put her feet up, and although she didn't mean to fall asleep, she woke up to find a blanket over her. And in spite of feeling that she shouldn't have slept, she knew that it was just as well that she had, for she had to go on duty that night, whether or not there was any news of a change in Mike's condition by then. And there was none.

Three times, Adam Brent had gone back to intensive care and each time, when he came out, he shook his head.

'No change, Kirsty,' he said the third time. 'He's holding his own, that's all I can say just now.'

Kirsty stood up, realising how cold and how stiff she was. 'I have to go,' she told him. 'I'm on duty. If—if there is anything, anything at all—'

'I'll let you know,' Adam Brent promised.

For the first time, now, she saw how weary and strained he was and she realised that he must have been called very early to operate on Mike. And then he had had his day's schedule in the theatre on top of that. And he might be called on again sometime during the night, either for Mike or for some other emergency patient.

'You're tired, Adam,' she said, without intending to, and only realising when she had said it that she had spoken as if the coolness and the misunderstandings between them had never happened, as if they were still friends. He smiled.

'Yes, I'm tired,' he admitted. 'So are you. But we've both got work to do.'

And work, Kirsty found, was the best possible thing for her. She couldn't forget about Mike and her anxiety for him, but there was a great deal to do on the ward and she was so busy that most of the time she could at least keep the thought of him submerged. She could at least keep up a reasonable pretence of being the efficient and professional Staff Nurse Kirsty Macrae, in charge of Harding ward and its patients through the night.

But of course, Sister Dawson knew about Mike, and so did Night Sister, and so did the juniors. Even the patients knew, Kirsty found eventually. When she looked in during the night to see if young Julie needed another pain-killer, she found the girl lying awake, her eyes fixed on the door.

'You should have rung, Julie,' she said, giving her her injection. 'There's no need for you to lie awake.'

Julie shook her head.

'I didn't mind,' she said. And then, her voice suddenly unsteady, 'I've been lying here watching you going up and down the ward, Nurse Macrae, looking after the patients, helping them. Cheering them up, when they needed it. And I keep thinking how awful it must be for you. I don't know how you can do it, when all the time you must be thinking about your boyfriend.'

Kirsty let the last word go.

'I can't do anything for Mike right now,' she said levelly. 'And there are plenty of people here needing me. Believe it or not, Julie, all you folks are helping me as much as I'm helping you.'

The girl lay back against her pillows. 'I suppose that's true,' she replied, obviously surprised. And then, a little drowsily, 'You know, Nurse Macrae, I think after I get out of here I'm going to see about training as a nurse. I was talking to Dr Brent about it and he said I shouldn't be foolish and get all soppy, because nursing needs a lot more than that. But he said, too, that he can see I'm tough, and he can see that when I make my mind up, I don't change. And I'm pretty sure I've made my mind up to be a nurse.'

'He's right, of course,' Kirsty agreed. 'You do have to think about it. But I could see you as a nurse, Julie.'

She left the girl, really drowsy now, and went back to the duty room. Twice during the night the telephone rang, and each time everything in Kirsty went completely still and as cold as ice. But there was no news of Mike, and no word from Adam Brent.

Sister Dawson, when she came on duty to take over from Kirsty, cast a swift, professional look at her staff nurse's face.

'Right, my girl,' she said, briskly. 'Go and have something to eat and then go to bed for at least four hours. You look dreadful. And you know as well as I do that you are likely to be pretty busy tonight, after operating day, so you'll need all your strength and all your energy.' And then, her voice softening, 'After that, you can go and see if there's any news. No, there's no use going now, I went there on my way to the ward, hoping I could tell you something. There's no change, my dear. Now, Nurse Macrae, please do as I say, for otherwise you'll be no use either to your patients or to your young man, when he does need you.'

'He isn't really my young man,' Kirsty said, but only half-heartedly, for that issue seemed of considerably less importance right now. 'All right, Sister, I'll do as you say.'

And she did, except as far as eating was concerned, for all at once it seemed impossible to make herself swallow anything. But she drank two cups of tea and went to bed, having set her alarm clock for four hours. She had to admit that she did feel better when she woke, had a quick shower, and then dressed and hurried over to the intensive care unit.

There were two people waiting there and she knew, without needing to be told, that they were Mike's parents. His father was an older version of Mike, but with dark eyes instead of the clear blue ones Mike had obviously inherited from his mother. Kirsty hesitated, but only for a moment. Then she went across the room to them.

'Are you Mike's parents?' she asked quietly. 'I'm Kirsty Macrae, a friend of Mike's.' Mike's mother, a small brown-haired woman, lifted her head.

'Kirsty?' she repeated. 'Mike has spoken about

you, my dear, he said he wanted to bring you some weekend to meet us. He—he—'

Her face crumpled, then, and she began to cry silently. Her husband put his arm around her and she turned her face against his shoulder.

'Is there any news?' Kirsty asked unevenly.

Mr Wilson shook his head. 'Nothing yet,' he said tiredly. 'I've just spoken to Dr Brent. He says they still daren't risk further surgery, or even assessment, until his condition stabilises. He suggested that I should take Mary back to her sister's in Wembley—we're staying there—so that we can get some rest. He says he'll get in touch with us immediately, if we're needed.'

His arm tightened around his wife and he looked at Kirsty doubtfully. 'I didn't feel we could, before—just felt that we had to be here, in case he comes round and wants us. But now that you're here, perhaps I should take the chance, for a few hours.'

Mike's mother had stopped crying now. 'I won't go,' she told her husband. 'I've got to be here, in case—in case—' Her voice faltered.

'I know how you feel, Mrs Wilson,' Kirsty said, keeping her voice steady. 'But if Dr Brent told you to go home and rest, he must feel there isn't anything you could do here in that time.' She thought for a moment. 'Look, instead of going to Wembley, why don't you go to Mike's flat? It's just round the corner. He shares it with Martin Low. I could get Martin's key for you. If you were staying there, you could get here in five minutes if anything happens.'

She managed to persuade Mike's parents to agree to this and went off to outpatients, where Martin Low was working, to get his key. Jane Farrant hurried over to her, but Kirsty told her why she was there and that there was no change.

When Mike's parents had gone, Kirsty sat down alone. She had a letter that had come from her parents the day before, and so she sat in the little waiting-room and read it. But somehow the glens and Invertorridon and the hospital news her mother had found to pass on to her, seemed to belong to a different world. In fact, Kirsty thought wearily, right now there seemed to be nothing and no one else in the world but this little room, and the room she could picture just along the corridor, where Mike lay unconscious.

Adam Brent, striding out of the lift and along the corridor, stopped when he saw her. 'We're taking him back to theatre,' he told her brusquely, and she could see that only half his attention was on her. 'Where are his parents?'

Kirsty told him that they had gone to Mike's flat and asked if she should call them. Adam shook his head.

'Not yet,' he said. 'Let's wait until we get him back here.' He looked at her and she saw that now he was really seeing her. 'We can't wait any longer,' he told her quietly. 'We may have to remove his spleen—we're pretty certain it's ruptured. And we'll have to assess any other damage at the same time. I'd rather have left him a little longer, but this gives me no choice.' Then he was gone, his green theatre-gown—for he had obviously come along in answer to an urgent summons—untied in his haste.

Once again, Kirsty waited. And now she was too tired and too worried even to close her eyes. Exhausted and tense, she sat on the edge of the seat. She saw the trolley being wheeled out of intensive care and across to theatre, the life-preserving drip attached to the still form, and part of her knew that this was Mike, while another part still wanted to deny any connection between the unconscious and critically-injured patient and the vital and laughing man she knew.

She didn't know how long it was before the trolley was wheeled back, but she could tell nothing from the masked and gowned figures attending. And it was perhaps another half hour before Adam Brent came out, still in his theatre-gown.

Kirsty stood up. 'Adam?' she said, her voice a thread. And then, remembering her training, 'Dr Brent?'

For a long time, it seemed to her, his dark eyes were unfocussed. She had the impression that he had some difficulty working out who she was. He came over to her.

'Kirsty, my dear, you've had a dreadful time,' he said, and the unlooked-for kindness in his voice brought the all-too-ready tears to her eyes.

'How did it go?' Kirsty asked him carefully.

'Better than I expected,' Adam said soberly. 'There was less damage from the ruptured spleen than I thought there would be. He's considerably better now.' He looked down at her. 'He's going to live, Kirsty.'

It was only because she was sensitive to every inflexion of his voice that she knew there was something more.

'But there's something else,' Kirsty said, and it wasn't a question.

'Yes, I'm afraid there is.' He was silent for a long time. 'There seems to be nerve damage to the spinal column. It looks as if he may not be able to walk again.'

CHAPTER EIGHT

THERE was pity in Adam Brent's dark eyes.

'What do you mean?' Kirsty asked him incredulously. She knew as she said it how foolish it was to ask this, for hadn't Adam just said, as plainly as it was possible to say, that there was a possibility that Mike wouldn't walk again?

But the surgeon didn't seem to find her question foolish. He took both her hands in his.

'Kirsty, my dear,' he said, gently, 'it looks as if he is going to be in a wheelchair.'

His hands tightened on hers, and even in this nightmare there was comfort for Kirsty in his reassurance. But Mike, in a wheelchair! It was an unbearable thought. And yet . . .

'At least he's alive,' she said, her voice low, and she pushed away the thought that perhaps Mike would rather not have survived, than be crippled and in a wheelchair. Suddenly, with a force that hurt her physically, she had a stabbing memory of him just a few days ago, jumping over the low gate outside the nurses' home when he came to collect her, and running towards her, his blue eyes laughing.

And the thought of that was all at once too much for her. She turned away from Adam—but not quickly enough, for he had seen that she was close to tears. He put his arm round her shoulders.

'Cry, Kirsty,' he told her. 'You've got a hard time ahead of you—don't try to keep control all the time, or you'll go to pieces.'

But she was beyond tears and she shook her head wordlessly. Adam stepped back and looked at her.

'I don't know whether this is the right time to say this, Kirsty,' he said quietly, 'but I have to say it. I'm sorry for the way I behaved to you, for the things I thought and let you see all too clearly I was thinking. I should have known that there must be more to Mike Wilson than I thought, for you to be in love with him. Since this happened, I've realised, from the way the other doctors speak about him— the way some of his patients speak about him—that I've seen only one side of him, and I've judged him rather harshly. I'm sorry about that, Kirsty. I'm not saying that I condone his behaviour in many ways, but I do want to say to you that I see now that I didn't really give him a chance. I'm sorry,' he said again.

Kirsty knew that it couldn't have been easy for Adam Brent to say this, to make this admission. But what had he said? *For you to be in love with him* . . .

She wanted, desperately, to tell him that she wasn't in love with Mike, that he was her dear friend and only that. Though why should it matter to Adam, who was engaged to Helen Conway, what her feelings were for Mike Wilson? It really seemed of little importance to clear up for him the way she felt about Mike, when Mike himself lay just along the corridor, still unconscious and not knowing, yet, how his life had changed.

'It's all right, Adam,' she said with difficulty. And then, remembering, she asked him, 'What about Mike's parents?'

'They've been sent for,' he told her, and his eyes were darker. 'I'll have to talk to them when they get here. But his mother has been given a sedative and she was better left undisturbed. Someone has gone to tell them, now that the operation is over.'

He went on speaking, but suddenly his voice was far away and Kirsty felt her forehead become damp. From a distance she heard Adam call her name urgently, but there was no fighting the waves of darkness. For a moment she felt Adam's arms holding her as she collapsed, and then there was nothing.

'All right, Kirsty, take it easy.'

She opened her eyes. Adam was there, still in his green theatre-gown, and one of the theatre nurses was there as well. Kirsty found that she was lying on the couch. She still felt shaky, but the dreadful feeling of distance had gone. The theatre nurse was looking at her with some curiosity and it suddenly dawned on Kirsty that this was anything but professional, one of the youngest staff nurses being carried to a couch by a surgical registrar! And also, she realised, he'd addressed her by her first name. She tried to sit up.

'I'm sorry, Dr Brent,' she said, not looking at him. 'I feel better now.'

'When did you last have something to eat, Kirsty? Probably not since young Wilson had his accident.'

'I can't remember,' Kirsty told him truthfully. Adam turned to the other nurse.

'Nurse Macrae has either been working on Harding or waiting here for news of Dr Wilson,' he told her. 'She's probably eaten very little in that time, quite apart from the worry of not knowing how things were going. Have you a junior over in theatre who could make some tea and toast for her?' He turned back to Kirsty. 'I presume you'll want to stay here until Mike's parents come?' He hesitated. 'There is really no point in anyone seeing him right now, he isn't likely to come round for a bit. But probably his mother will want to.'

Kirsty answered his unspoken question. 'I'll wait,' she told him. 'I'd rather see him when he's conscious.'

Adam nodded. 'I'm going now, Kirsty, but I'll see you. And take care. You won't do yourself or your young man any good if you don't look after yourself. You know as well as I do that he's going to need all the help and support he can get.'

He left then, and the nurse from theatre went as well. Five minutes later a younger nurse brought Kirsty a tray with tea and two slices of toast. Obediently, because Adam had told her to, she ate the toast and drank the tea. She had just finished when Mike's parents came in, and she could see right away that they knew.

'Have you seen Mike?' his mother asked unsteadily. 'I want to see him, even if he doesn't know me. I want to see my boy.'

'He won't be conscious yet, Mary,' Mr Wilson told her. 'You know Dr Brent said that. And you mustn't go in there upset.' He looked at Kirsty. 'Dr Brent was waiting for us downstairs,' he said quietly. 'He told us. He said we could look at Mike, but that's all, at the moment. Have you been in?'

Kirsty shook her head and her heart went out to the two weary, bewildered and shaken people.

'No, I'll wait,' she replied. And then, her training coming uppermost, 'Dr Brent would tell you that even if Mike seems to be unconscious you should try to be as calm as possible. You can never tell the level of understanding a patient has, recovering from an anaesthetic.'

'I won't upset him,' Mrs Wilson said, and her obvious and careful composure brought a blur of tears to Kirsty's eyes. 'I just want to see him.'

Kirsty waited until they came out again, in a short time. Mike's mother was crying, but she looked at Kirsty though her tears and her voice was quite steady.'

'He's alive, and that's what really matters,' she said. 'As for the—the walking, you never know. I just don't believe my Mike is going to spend the rest of his life in a wheelchair.'

Kirsty's eyes met Mike's father's eyes.

'You must be realistic, Mary, love,' he said to her gently.

'Yes, I'll be realistic,' his wife replied. 'But I won't give up hope. *We'll* keep on hoping, won't we, Kirsty?' She came across the room now to Kirsty. 'My dear, we've so much wanted to meet you. I—I wish it could have been in different circumstances, but I want to tell you now that it means a great deal to me, and to Mike's father, to think of you sitting here waiting all this time. I just told the nurse in that intensive care room that I want Mike's girl allowed in any time it's possible, because I just know it will help him so much to see you.'

Kirsty felt a moment's panic. First Adam, and now Mike's mother! She wanted, desperately, to say that she would gladly see Mike, but she wasn't his *girl*. Only his friend.

But she couldn't say it. Not with Mike's mother looking at her with eyes the same clear blue as Mike's own. And so she said nothing.

Jane Farrant agreed, when they talked about it the next day, that there was nothing else Kirsty could have done.

'I can see that,' she admitted. 'I mean, here's Mike just been operated on, you barely know that he's going to live, and you hear that he isn't going to walk again. I agree it isn't the best time to go pointing out that you and Mike are just good friends. It does seem pretty irrelevant in the circumstances. But,' her blue eyes clouded, 'I don't think I like it, Kirsty. If this hadn't happened, you would already have talked to Mike, wouldn't you? You'd already have got the whole situation clear with him.'

Kirsty sighed.

'Yes, I would,' she agreed. 'But it didn't work out that way, and I really don't see what else I can do. And it isn't doing me any harm, Jane, to have everyone think I'm Mike's girl.'

The thought was there, as she said it—because the only person she would really want to know the truth wouldn't care in any case. She stood up.

'Thanks for collecting my uniforms from the laundry,' she said.

'Andrea did it—got mine for me too,' her friend told her. 'She's a good kid, and on her way to becoming a good nurse. Kirsty—you're not on duty for an hour still.'

'I know,' Kirsty replied. 'I'm going over to see if I can see Mike.'

She put her cloak on and, because it was raining, went along the underground passage that connected the nurses' home with the hospital. She knew that she should have been along earlier to the intensive care unit to see Mike, for she had had a phone call from his father to say that he had recovered consciousness enough to recognise them.

Somewhat to her own surprise, she was finding in herself a strange reluctance to go and see Mike lying in a hospital bed, attached to a monitoring machine, with a drip set up. Through her years of training, and since she qualified, she should have become accustomed to seeing patients like that. But this wasn't just a patient, this was Mike. Mike, who wasn't going to be able to get up out of that bed and walk again. Mike, who would leave the hospital in a wheelchair.

'Only a few minutes,' the sister in charge warned her as she took her into the monitoring room where Mike was. At the door, she looked at Kirsty. 'You'll realise, of course, Nurse,' she said quietly, 'that so far all he knows is that he's been in an accident? Those are Dr Brent's instructions at the moment.'

Kirsty had often pictured Mike lying white and still, but in spite of that the reality was so much worse that she felt her breath catch in her throat. His eyes were closed and she sat down beside him quietly, meaning just to stay there for a very short time and then slip out. But after a moment he opened his eyes and looked at her.

'Kirsty?' he murmured, and she had to lean closer to hear him. 'Are you looking after me?'

She shook her head. 'Only visiting,' she told him. He glanced around.

'I'm in intensive care?' he asked her.

'Yes, you are,' she told him steadily. 'Mike, I can't stay long, I'm on duty. But I'll be back.'

'Give me your hand,' he murmured, and when she put her hand on his, she was surprised at the strength he managed to find. 'Now you can't go,' he told her, and even in the weakness of his voice there was satisfaction, just as, unbelievably, there was a gleam of laughter in his blue eyes.

'I'll stay for a little,' she promised him, and she sat quietly until his breathing became deeper and his hand loosened its hold on hers. Gently, she slipped her hand free and stood up. And for the first time she saw that Adam Brent must have come into the room so quietly that she hadn't heard him. He was standing watching, his lean brown face still, his eyes unreadable.

'Oh, I didn't know you were there,' Kirsty said, annoyed at herself for being unable to hide her confusion. 'I, I'm just going.'

He came out into the corridor with her.

'I'm sure your visit did him good,' he said. 'You know as well as I do, Kirsty, how important it is for anyone to have the support and the company of the people close to him at a time like this. And it's going to be even more important for Mike Wilson, when we have to tell him. It won't be too long before her starts wondering and asking questions. Questions I will have to answer truthfully.'

At the end of the corridor he stopped and looked down at her.

'It's a heavy load for you to carry, Kirsty,' he said, and the kindness in his voice made her throat tighten. 'Nursing in itself is demanding, emotionally as well as physically, and it can't be easy for you, having this as well.'

Warm sympathy from Adam Brent was almost more than Kirsty could take, and she was glad when his voice changed, became professional as he told her he'd probably be looking in at Harding some time during the evening, to check on an ulcer patient he had just operated on. 'She's had a tough time—I've left instructions, but keep an eye on her.'

As soon as possible after going on duty, Kirsty went to have a look at Adam's ulcer patient. She was a woman of fifty, Kirsty saw from her notes, and the operation had had to be done sooner than had originally been planned, as her condition had deteriorated. But the operation itself had been successful, it seemed, and the woman's condition had now stabilised.

In spite of that, there was something that bothered Kirsty about this Mrs Masters. She took her pulse, checked her dressings, adjusted the drip, and when Adam came up to the ward an hour later, she told him all that had been done, and gave him his patient's chart.

'Thanks, Nurse,' Adam said formally, scanning it quickly. 'Yes, everything seems to be all right.' And then, taking her by surprise, 'But you're not happy about her?'

It was a moment before Kirsty answered.

'No, I'm not,' she admitted with reluctance. 'As you say, everything is as it should be. And yet something bothers me.'

'A hunch?' Adam asked, smiling, but his eyes were thoughtful. 'Or Highland second sight?'

'I'm not sure,' Kirsty said slowly, feeling foolish and unprofessional. Adam looked down at her.

'I've had these feelings myself,' he said at last, abruptly. 'And it's surprising how often they've been right. I'm on call if you need me.'

He nodded and strode off down the corridor, leaving Kirsty ridiculously pleased that he hadn't thought her too foolish, that he was prepared to admit that there could be reason for anxiety even when there was nothing specific to justify it.

Kirsty and her juniors did the half-hourly pulse readings that Adam had instructed, and just before midnight Kirsty decided to make these quarter-hourly, although there was plenty to do on the ward. The next time she checked, she knew that her feeling had been right. Mrs Master's pulse was racing, and in the fifteen minutes since the last check she had gone a greyish colour.

'Call Dr Brent,' Kirsty told her junior in a low, urgent voice, 'and then get back here stat.'

But even before the younger girl had returned, the woman in the bed had haemorrhaged, swiftly and dramatically. Kirsty, who hadn't really known what she was expecting, was nevertheless ready to deal with any emergency, and five minutes later, when Adam Brent strode down the ward, she had things under control. Adam took in the situation immediately and he and Kirsty worked together with barely a word exchanged.

An hour later, with a new drip set up and a second pint of blood running smoothly through the transfusion apparatus, Mrs Masters was deathly pale, but the awful greyness had gone from her face.

'She'll do,' Adam said wearily, standing looking down at her. 'Leave the screens around her bed. If you can give me a chair, I'll sit here for a bit.' He smiled at her, faintly. 'No, it isn't my turn to have a hunch, just that I'd be happier to do that.'

Kirsty brought him an armchair from one of the side wards, and then she went back to the duty room and made coffee. She carried Adam's down

the ward to him and he thanked her for it, his eyes
and obviously most of his attention still on his
patient.

Through the rest of the night, as Kirsty worked,
she glanced in. Each time Adam, although
obviously very tired, looked up and smiled briefly.
It was after six before Mrs Masters came round,
recognising Adam and obviously reassured to see
him there, and then fell asleep. Adam left the ward
just as the day staff came to take over.

'Quite a night you've had, Nurse Macrae,' Sister
Dawson said, her keen eyes taking everything
in. 'But you seem to have coped reasonably
well.'

This was high praise, and it sustained Kirsty as
she finished handing over, collected her cloak and
went off duty. She was tired and suddenly realised
that she was also hungry, but the thought of the
crowded canteen held no appeal for her and she
went out the front door instead of going there,
thinking she might just make some tea and toast in
the flat.

'Kirsty.'

She looked round, startled, to see Adam Brent
sitting in his car, which was parked just beside the
entrance.

'You look like a zombie,' he told her. 'Why
aren't you going for breakfast? I don't suppose you
were off at all last night.'

'I wasn't,' Kirsty admitted. 'But I couldn't face
the canteen.'

'Neither could I,' Adam said. He held the door

open. 'Get in and I'll take you for breakfast to a little place I know. It's just five minutes away.'

She hesitated.

'Come on, you're tired and hungry and so am I,' Adam said, and the impatience in his voice was so unusual that Kirsty found herself obeying meekly.

'Much better than the canteen, you must agree,' he said to her an hour later, when their plates were cleared away and their coffee-cups refilled.

Kirsty looked around her. It wasn't a big place and there were very few people in it, but there was something pleasant and restful about the atmosphere. The blue gingham tablecloths and curtains were pleasantly informal and the breakfast had been delicious.

'Nice place,' she agreed. Until now, tiredness and hunger had prevented her from realising that she was sitting here alone with Adam. The confusion of this thought—and her own reactions to it—brought a warm colour to her cheeks, and she was all too conscious of this. 'Thank you for bringing me here,' she said quickly. 'I must get back now.'

He was looking at her, and there was something in his dark eyes that made her strangely uncomfortable.

'It's a favourite place of mine,' he told her. 'I thought you'd like it.'

A 'favourite place—and no doubt, Kirsty thought, with an ache that shook her, he brings Helen Conway here. No doubt they've often sat at this very table together.

She finished her coffee and stood up. Adam put his own cup down and helped her on with her cloak. His car was parked at the back, in a small parking area, and they went out the back door and into the car.

'You're tired, Kirsty,' he said, and the unexpected gentleness of his voice shook her.

'Och, it's nothing,' she said quickly. 'A few hours' sleep and I'll be fine.'

'You're working too hard,' he told her, still unexpectedly.

She shook her head. 'I enjoy it,' she told him with complete truth.

He smiled. 'You're such a little thing,' he said, and her heart treacherously turned over.

'I may be wee,' she said quickly, 'but I'm very strong.'

She didn't think he was listening to her. He was looking at her, his eyes very dark, his mouth unsmiling, and when he murmured her name she could hardly hear him for the thudding of her own heart, fast and uneven.

'Kirsty—oh, Kirsty.'

Afterwards, she could never decide which of them moved first—but she was in his arms and his lips were on hers, warm and demanding. And this time it was the kiss she had dreamed of, a kiss with all the tenderness and all the passion she had longed for from the moment she had met Adam Brent.

CHAPTER NINE

'KIRSTY, Kirsty,' Adam said, unsteadily.

And instead of releasing her, he kissed her again. Afterwards, thinking of his kiss, reliving it, Kirsty knew with complete certainty that if they had been somewhere else, neither she nor Adam could have stopped there.

But they were in Adam's car in the car-park behind the little restaurant, five minutes from the hospital. And so they drew apart at last.

'Please, don't say you're sorry, Adam,' Kirsty said quickly, seeing that he was about to speak. He was still very close to her.

'I'm not sorry,' he told her, his voice low. 'I've wanted to do that for a long time—longer even than I would admit to myself. No, Kirsty, I'm not sorry, but I shouldn't have done it. You know that as well as I do.'

Helen Conway, with Adam's ring on her left hand, appeared before Kirsty's dazed eyes.

'Yes, I know that, Adam,' she replied, and she was unable to keep the sadness from her voice.

'I'll take you back now,' he shook himself and started the car. He said nothing as he drove the short distance to the hospital, but when he stopped he turned to her. 'That was an interlude, Kirsty,' he said, with difficulty. 'It won't happen again.'

'I know, Adam,' Kirsty replied forlornly. And then, because she couldn't bear to see him looking so unhappy, she tried to smile. 'It's all right, you know,' she said gently.

'Is it?' Adam asked her, looking straight ahead of him. 'Kirsty, I wish we could go back to that time in Invertorridon. I wish—' And then, with an effort that hurt her to see, he stopped himself. 'But that's foolish,' he said, and she wondered whether he was speaking to her or to himself. 'There's no going back.'

For a moment he took both her hands in his. 'Look after yourself, Kirsty.'

When he had gone and Kirsty was in her room alone, she thought that there had almost been a goodbye in the way he said that. And of course, she reminded herself, that was how it should be, with Adam engaged to Helen Conway.

He'd been tired, that was all, and all his defences down. I am not deceiving myself, she thought, when I think that there is an attraction, at the very least, between us. Perhaps, if Adam wasn't engaged to Helen Conway . . .

But he was, and he obviously regarded his engagement as an impossible barrier between them, she reminded herself. For a moment, with a bitterness that was unlike her usual self, Kirsty found herself wondering if Adam knew anything about the way Helen Conway behaved when they weren't together. More than once, Jane had come home from a party and mentioned that Helen had been there, and each time without Adam, for he had been on call.

But he chose her, Kirsty reminded herself steadily. He asked her to marry him, and he must love her. And it is none of my business to be worrying and wondering about how things are between the two of them.

Determinedly, she put Adam Brent and the girl he was engaged to out of her mind. She would sleep, she decided, for she was very tired, and she would get up in time to go and see Mike before she went on duty again.

Mike was very much better, she found, and although he was still very weak, she could see such an improvement from the day before that she wasn't surprised when he told her he was to be moved out of intensive care.

'I asked them to put me in your ward,' he told her, 'but they thought the excitement might be a bit much for the lady patients!'

'Not to mention the nurses,' Kirsty agreed. 'I'm thinking I'd have trouble with my young student nurses, Mike, if you were there.'

Behind the teasing and the bantering her heart ached, for she knew that it couldn't be long before he would have to be told. And she knew, too, that until it was done, until Mike had accepted it, she would have to let things be and say nothing. It seemed such a heartless thing to be doing, to come and visit him and say—I'm sorry things are so bad with you, Mike, I'm sorry you're going to be in a wheelchair, and by the way, I would like to make it clear that I'm only visiting you as a friend, I just want you to understand that that is all there is between you and me . . .

No, she couldn't do it. Not yet.

'Kirsty?' Mike said, a little drowsily. 'You're miles away. If you're worrying about me, I'm all right. I gather it was pretty dicey for a bit, but I don't bow out that easily. And I'm giving you fair warning now—by the time I get out of here, I'm making no guarantees about that promise to behave myself!'

For a moment there was something in his eyes that made her wonder if he could possibly know. Then it was gone, and she told herself she must have imagined it.

'You're sleepy,' she told him firmly. 'Don't try to speak. I'll sit here for a wee while before I go on duty.'

'They keep giving me pills and injections,' he said, his voice blurred.

She sat with him until he fell asleep, and then she drew her hand away from him and went out. As she was leaving the intensive care unit she met his mother and father coming in.

'How is he?' Mrs Wilson asked her eagerly.

'Better than he was yesterday, by a long way,' Kirsty told her honestly. She told them he was to be taken out of intensive care. 'So they must feel happier about him.' Her tongue somehow refused to say Adam's name.

Slowly, the momentary brightness faded from Mike's mother's face. She looked up at her husband.

'I think we will have to stay here until they've told him,' she said quietly.

'Yes, we'll do that,' he agreed. He turned to Kirsty. 'We'll have to go home soon. I have to get back to work, and if Mary is to be needed near Mike, we'll have to organise something.' He was trying very hard to be practical and unemotional and Kirsty's heart went out to him. 'I suppose there will be physiotherapy afterwards?'

'I should think so,' Kirsty replied. 'You'd have to ask Dr Brent about that.'

'One thing, Kirsty, dear,' Mike's mother said then. 'When we do go, we'll feel so much happier to know that you're here with Mike. Come along, Jim, let's get in and see him, even if he is asleep.'

When they had gone, Kirsty stood in the corridor waiting for the lift, her heart heavy at the realisation that so much was taken for granted by Mike's parents. And yet she couldn't feel resentful, for how were they to know?

Once again she was glad that Harding ward was busy, glad that she was kept occupied through the long night hours, glad that there was little time for thinking. She saw little of Adam in the next few nights, and when he did come to the ward in the evening to check on his patients he was professional and impersonal. And that, Kirsty reminded herself, was how he should be.

But three days after Mike was moved from intensive care, Kirsty, on her way back to the nurses' home after coming off duty, found Adam waiting for her. And in spite of all the things she had told herself, there was a moment of sheer physical impact that left her breathless. But this was Adam Brent the surgical registrar, and not the Adam Brent who had held her in his arms and kissed her.

'I've just been talking to Mike Wilson,' he told her quietly. 'He came right out and asked me if he would walk again, and I had to tell him it was unlikely. He'd suspected that something was wrong, but he thought it was post-accident trauma. This morning he asked me. I wanted you to know, before you go to see him.'

Now he really looked at her. 'You look exhausted, Kirsty,' he said, and she thought that she couldn't bear the concern in his voice. 'But perhaps you would like to go and see him now, just for a few minutes. I told Sister to let you in if you came.'

Kirsty felt that the last thing in the world she wanted was to go and see Mike when he had just been given this news. And when she herself was not only worn out, but shaken by the realisation, once again, of the effect Adam Brent had on her. But she knew that she had to go.

Mike was staring up at the ceiling. She sat down beside him and took his hand in hers, but he didn't look at her.

'Wheelchair doctor,' he said at last, slowly. 'How do you feel about that, Kirsty?'

'How do you feel about it, Mike?' she asked him.

Now he turned and looked at her, and the bitterness she had expected was there in his clear blue eyes, in the tight line of his jaw.

'Damned angry,' he told her. 'Because some idiot jumped the traffic-lights.'

'I'm glad you feel angry,' Kirsty said firmly. 'I'd much rather see you feeling angry than hopeless. Anger will get you somewhere.'

'Twice round the course in the next paraplegics' race?' he asked her.

And then, with no warning, he was crying. Kirsty knelt beside him and held him while he wept, saying nothing, only holding him. When he stopped, she dried his face and then sponged it.

'All right,' he said, when she had finished. 'That's that. I've got it out of my system, and thanks for being here, Kirsty.'

As the days went by, Kirsty saw, with an admiration she hadn't expected to feel, that Mike had meant just what he said. He refused to be sorry for himself and he concentrated fiercely on learning to do whatever he could do.

'Adam Brent and the physiotherapist are having to hold him back,' Kirsty told Jane Farrant. 'He is quite determined to be as independent as possible. It's an old-fashioned word, Jane, but he's very gallant about it, gallant and full of courage.'

'And because of that, you can't bring yourself to tell him how you feel?' Jane asked. Kirsty flushed.

'I know,' she said. 'I can't let it go on. It just doesn't seem the right time now. I mean, his parents have gone, he's depending on me.'

Jane shrugged.

'You're not just going to abandon him,' she pointed out. 'You'll still be visiting him, you'll still be his friend.' Her vivid blue eyes held Kirsty's steadily. 'But you don't think that will be enough for Mike?'

'I don't know,' Kirsty admitted. 'It just seems a bit of a low-down time to tell him. Oh, Jane, I wish so much now that I'd told him before. If I had, I could have been visiting him purely as a friend now and it would have been fine.' Jane stood up.

'Tell you what, Kirsty,' she said casually, 'I'll pop in and see him too, whenever I can, and I'll pass the word around that he can have visitors now. We'll all cheer him up and maybe before too long you'll find he can take it in his stride.' She stopped, and for the first time in the months Kirsty had known her, she looked stricken. 'That wasn't the best way to put it,' she said after a moment. 'I'd better watch myself if I'm going to visit Mike.'

Jane was as good as her word and she began to visit Mike regularly, and so did some more of his friends. The following month, Kirsty was back on day duty, which meant that she had less chance to go and see Mike during the day. But Jane was on nights, and between them and other friends there were few days when Mike's new wheelchair wasn't pushed around the hospital garden if the weather was good enough.

Once, when Kirsty decided to use her tea-break to look in on him, the ward sister told her that he was out in the garden. Kirsty hurried out, expecting to find Jane with him. But the young doctor pushing the wheelchair was another friend of Mike's— Steve Hartley. And walking beside them was Helen

Conway, Adam's fiancée. Kirsty remembered now that this was the young doctor Helen had been with once before when she had seen her at a party.

'Kirsty!' Mike said, his face lighting up. 'You know Steve, don't you? And Helen?'

Helen Conway's blonde head turned towards Kirsty.

'Oh yes,' she said coolly. 'Adam's little Scottish nurse.'

I am not Adam's little Scottish nurse, Kirsty thought furiously, and she hoped that her smile in return was as cool and as self-possessed as Helen's own.

Helen turned back to Mike.

'I believe you and Adam are bosom buddies now, Mike?' she asked, smiling.

'I wouldn't say that,' Mike replied, and he smiled as well, his eyes meeting Kirsty's. 'I think Adam still feels I was a pretty bad influence on too many of the nurses around Luke's.'

'Adam needs to learn how to have fun,' Helen said lightly, and Kirsty was shaken by the wave of anger that flooded her whole body. 'I must admit I didn't realise how hard it would be to get him to forget his patients even for a little while.' She patted Steve Hartley's cheek and the diamond on her left hand shone in the sunshine. 'He could learn a thing or two from you, Steve, couldn't he? And from Mike.'

'Leave me out of it,' Mike said quietly. 'I'm not exactly in the fun stakes right now.'

It was so seldom that she had heard the bleakness

there was now in his voice, that Kirsty looked at him, taken aback. And then, after a moment, Mike recovered and began to ask Steve about another young doctor who had gone to America.

I forget, Kirsty thought with compassion. Because Mike is always so cheerful, so positive, so determined to make the best of things, I forget that there must be times when things get him down.

'I'll have to go,' she said now, looking at the watch pinned on her uniform. 'This is just my tea-break. I'll have to let Sister go off for hers now.'

'You should come and work for me in theatre, Kirsty,' Helen Conway said, unexpectedly. 'I hear from Adam that you're very good—I could do with a capable and enthusiastic staff nurse on my team.' She turned. 'I've just been talking about you, darling,' she said lightly. 'I'm trying to persuade Kirsty to come and work in theatre.'

'Kirsty's doing fine in Harding,' Adam said, not looking at her. 'I don't know what Sister Dawson would do without her.' He turned to Mike. 'I see you've got plenty of company, Mike—I just dropped by to tell you that Cameron from Edinburgh is going to have a look at you in a couple of days. He'll be down here for a conference and I've asked him to come and see you. All right with you?'

'All right with me,' Mike replied evenly, but Kirsty knew there was suppressed excitement in his voice. 'Just having a look?'

'Just that,' Adam agreed, his voice as casual as Mike's own. But for a moment his eyes met Mike's and he smiled, acknowledging the hope that neither of them were prepared to put into words. For Mr Cameron, Kirsty knew, was an orthopaedic specialist of world renown. And if Adam thought it was worthwhile asking him to have a look at Mike . . .

'I'll be late,' she said, quickly. 'Sorry, Mike—see you tomorrow.'

'Sure, Kirsty,' Mike replied. 'Hey, don't go knocking my doctor over!'

Kirsty, whirling round, hadn't seen that Adam Brent had moved. He caught her arm to steady her, and for a moment, in the hospital garden, with his hand on her arm, Kirsty was back in the car with him, trying to recover from his kiss. The kiss she had tried so hard to forget. And she knew, as his hand tightened on her arm, that he too was thinking of that moment.

Abruptly, Adam dropped his hand. And Kirsty, her chin held high and her cheeks warm, hurried out of the garden and back into the hospital. But just before she was out of earshot she heard Helen Conway's voice, light and caressing, 'Adam, darling, you're not going to tell me you're working tonight?'

Kirsty hurried back to her ward, glad to be kept busy doing the patients' teas while Sister went off for half an hour. She was glad to be forced to have no time to think of Mike and the bleakness in his voice, or Helen Conway, her hand touching Steve Hartley's cheek. And most of all, of Adam.

There was a patient to be catheterised and Kirsty

worked gently and swiftly, explaining what she was doing and reassuring the anxious woman that this would be no more than a temporary measure. After that she had to adjust a drip when the intravenous therapy had caused tissuing, and then there were injections to be done. All too soon the day ended and it was time to hand over to the night staff. Kirsty went back to her flat, telling herself that she would spend some time helping young Andrea with her notes for her anatomy exam which was coming up soon.

'You don't go out at all just now,' Jane had said the night before. 'If you're not visiting Mike, you're helping Andrea. Look, I'm off on Friday—come along with me, there's a crowd of us going out.'

'I don't feel like it, but thanks for the thought, Jane,' Kirsty said honestly. Jane's blue eyes clouded.

'You're not making things any easier for yourself, you know,' she said abruptly. 'And in a way, you're not making things easier for Mike. He knows you don't go out—he's bound to think it's because you'd rather just be with him.' And then, with her usual swift change of mood, 'Sorry, Kirsty pet, I know you're working things out in your own way, I should leave it to you.'

Two nights later, when Kirsty went off duty she found a note in her pigeonhole at the nurses' home. It was short, almost abrupt.

'Hamish Cameron has seen Mike Wilson today. I'd like to talk to you when you come off duty. Please ring me. Adam Brent.'

Kirsty went upstairs and changed before she rang Adam at the number he had given her on his note. His voice was impersonal, businesslike, as he said he would be outside the nurses' home in half an hour. Kirsty went to the dining-room and had some cold meat and salad and a quick cup of coffee before going out to meet him. To her surprise, he didn't have his car.

'It's warm, we'll go across to the park,' he said, taking her agreement for granted. He said nothing more until they were across the busy street and into the surprising quiet of the park. Then he turned to her.

'Hamish Cameron saw Mike today,' he said quietly. 'He has spoken to him, and I wanted to tell you what he plans to do.'

'To do?' Kirsty asked him. 'You mean he thinks he can do something?

'He's going to try,' Adam told her. 'He is going to operate, using a new technique that is really only experimental. Mike Wilson knows this, and he has agreed.'

'What are the chances?' Kirsty asked. Adam shrugged.

'Fifty-fifty, perhaps less,' he said. 'But it's a chance, and Mike is prepared to take it. I thought it could help him if you were in the picture as well. You see, if the operation is unsuccessful Cameron will have to do a fusing, and that could leave Mike with even less mobility than he has now.' Kirsty looked at him.

'It's Mike's decision to make,' she said quietly.

Adam Brent looked straight ahead.

'Yours, too,' he replied. 'You may feel you'd rather leave things as they are. Mike's condition at the moment makes marriage a more acceptable proposition than it will be if the operation is unsuccessful.'

Kirsty felt all the colour drain from her cheeks and she knew that now she had to make her own feelings clear, first to Adam, and then to Mike himself.

'Adam,' she said unsteadily, 'you don't understand. There isn't any question of marriage. Mike and I—we've had fun together, but it never was serious.' And then, with painful honesty, she said, 'At least it never was on my side. I was—I was going to tell him this, and then he had the accident and I didn't feel it was right. But Adam, I haven't ever had any intention of letting Mike think that I would marry him!'

Adam Brent stopped. He looked down at her and she saw, with a shock, that he was very angry.

'I wouldn't have thought this of you, Kirsty,' he said coldly. 'To ditch him, because he's in a wheel-chair! That's hitting a man when he's down. Sure, there are plenty of girls who couldn't take it, but I thought you were the faithful kind, the loyal kind.'

Kirsty put her hand on his arm, hardly able to believe that this was happening. 'Adam,' she said desperately, 'you don't understand.'

His eyes were very dark and very remote.

'I'm afraid I understand all too well,' he replied.

'I don't think there's much point in me saying anything more.'

And once again, as he had done before, he walked away from her.

CHAPTER TEN

ADAM BRENT was out of sight, but still Kirsty stood there alone, hardly able to take in what had just happened.

All she had tried to do was to explain to him just how things were between Mike and her—to make it clear to him that there never had been any question of them marrying. Perhaps, she thought painfully now, she had hoped that he would be able to help her to find the right way to tell Mike.

But he had misunderstood completely. He thought that she was running out on Mike because he was in a wheelchair. He thought . . . And now Kirsty remembered something else.

That morning when Adam had kissed her in his car behind the little restaurant, he had said to her that he wasn't sorry because he had wanted to kiss her. *I shouldn't have done it*, he had said. *You know that as well as I do.*

And Kirsty, thinking of Helen Conway with Adam's ring on her left hand, had accepted that. But she saw now, all too clearly, that Adam had been thinking of what he saw as *her* commitments just as much as his own.

I thought you were the faithful kind, the loyal kind, he had said.

Kirsty walked slowly along the deserted paths of the park.

I *am* the faithful kind, and the loyal kind, Adam, she thought with desolation. I'm faithful to you, and I'd be loyal to you, if only I had the chance. But faithfulness and loyalty aren't enough without love. If I had loved Mike, if I had committed myself to him, nothing would have come between us. It wouldn't have mattered if he'd been in a wheelchair for the rest of his life.

It hurt unbelievably that Adam thought she was the kind of girl who wouldn't stand by her man. And yet, slowly, painfully, Kirsty tried to see it as Adam must have seen it. With reluctance, she had to admit that it did all add up—what he had seen of the relationship before the accident could certainly have led him to think they were in love.

But Adam should have known, Kirsty thought stubbornly. He should have known that if I had loved Mike, I would have stood by him all the way. And he should have known, too, that if I had loved Mike, I would never have let him kiss me the way he did that morning.

A warm tide of colour flooded her face at the memory of her response to Adam's kiss and of what he must have thought of her afterwards. So many misunderstandings between the two of them! The weight of it all hung heavily in Kirsty's heart. But there was nothing she could do, she knew that, to change the way Adam Brent thought of her.

Mike's operation was scheduled for two days later. He was tense and strained and it was obvious that he could think of little else but the very limited chance of success.

'Do you think I'm right, Kirsty,' he asked her more than once, 'to tell them to go ahead on such a small chance?'

But here Kirsty held firm. She had done enough harm, she felt, by not having the courage to make her own feelings clear. She wasn't prepared to do any more.

'I'm sorry, Mike,' she told him quietly, 'but it's your decision. No one else can make it for you.' All the laughter had gone from his blue eyes.

'You know that if it isn't successful, I'll have even less mobility than I have now?' he asked her.

'Yes, I know,' Kirsty replied. And she said it again. 'It's your decision, Mike.'

For a moment there was a shadow in his eyes and she wondered if he knew what she wanted to say to him—what she would have to say to him, whichever way the operation went. Perhaps, she thought, it would be better said now, so that he would know her decision wasn't affected by the success or the failure of the operation.

'Mike,' she said, slowly, not sure how she could go on, 'I've been thinking—'

'Dangerous pastime,' Mike replied, his voice light again, although to Kirsty it was a forced lightness. 'You might do yourself some harm, Kirsty!'

No, she thought, I can't say it now. Not until the operation is over.

She saw him briefly just before the operation.

His parents were with him but he had had his pre-med and was already drowsy.

'Good luck, Mike,' Kirsty murmured, and she kissed his cheek.

'Better wish the surgeon good luck too,' Mike replied, with an attempt at his old jauntiness that made Kirsty's heart ache.

She was glad that she was on duty while the operation was being done, for the thought of waiting along the corridor from the operating-theatre, with his parents, was unbearable.

'It's going to be quite a long one,' Kirsty reminded them before she left to go to the ward. 'You should go out and get some fresh air.'

Mrs Wilson shook her head and Kirsty thought that there were more grey hairs than there had been a few weeks ago, when she had seen both of them for the first time.

'I want to be right here,' she said firmly. And then, her hand on Kirsty's arm, 'Will you be able to come back here to find out how things have gone?'

'Yes, I'll be back,' Kirsty told her. 'I've asked for an early lunch-time, so I should be back about the time they finish in the theatre.'

In fact, Mike's parents were still waiting when she got there, and there was no news. Kirsty arranged for a tray of tea and some sandwiches and she could see that it was as much an effort for them to eat anything as it was for her.

It was almost time for her to go back on duty when the door opened and Adam Brent, still in his green theatre-gown, came through with the orthopaedic surgeon, Mr Cameron. They both looked very tired, Kirsty thought. For a moment Adam's eyes met hers and then, quite deliberately she thought, he turned to Mike's parents.

'Mr Cameron will tell you how things went,' he said to them, and Kirsty, because she knew this man so well, in spite of everything there had been between them, knew that the operation had been successful. She listened as the Edinburgh surgeon explained what he had done and that the operation had been as successful as he had hoped.

'You mean he'll walk again?' Mike's father asked, almost unable to believe the news.

'I mean just that, Mr Wilson,' the surgeon replied. 'It will take time, and he's going to need a lot of physiotherapy, and he will have to accept that there will be some things he won't be able to ask that back of his to do. But yes, he'll walk again.'

Mrs Wilson was crying and Kirsty hugged her briefly and said she had to go back on duty. At the door of the waiting-room Adam Brent looked down at her.

'I'm sure you're pleased to know that the operation was successful,' he said coolly. 'Or does it make any difference?'

'It doesn't make any difference,' Kirsty replied, sick at heart for the way he was looking at her.

And it didn't, she thought as she went back to the ward. Perhaps it would make it easier for her to tell Mike, now that she knew that he wasn't going to spend the rest of his life in a wheelchair. But she would have had to tell him, no matter what the result had been, for she could not have lived with a lie. And it would have been a lie to let him think that she loved him. There was still the question of finding the right time though, and there was never a right time for bad news.

It would have to be done, she knew, before Mike left the hospital. He was to spend a few weeks at home and then he was to go to the hospital annexe, where he would have intensive daily physiotherapy.

'I gather you haven't said anything to Mike yet,' Jane said to her one night when they were drinking hot chocolate before going to bed. 'You plan on doing it soon?'

'Yes, before he goes,' Kirsty replied. Jane's blue eyes were level and direct.

'You haven't changed your mind? I mean, you haven't found that the way Mike has reacted to all this has made you feel differently about him?'

Kirsty looked at her friend. 'What do you mean?' she asked. Jane coloured.

'Just that it seems to me Mike has shown himself to be quite a guy through all this. I just wondered if you'd been thinking the same.'

'Yes, I think he's been terrific,' Kirsty agreed slowly. 'I feel very proud to be his friend, and I respect him for the courage he's had, but—'

'But you don't love him,' Jane said.

'No, I don't love him,' Kirsty replied sadly, and she thought, not for the first time, that in many ways it would have been simpler all round if she had. 'I'm just putting off telling him.'

'He won't fall apart, you know,' Jane said, and Kirsty looked at her friend in surprise. 'He's tough, Mike, in many ways. I—I know how he feels about you, but I think you're underestimating him. Sure, he'll mind, but—Kirsty, Mike isn't the sort of man to be happy with second best, and that's what it would be, wouldn't it?'

Second best. Kirsty thought for one stabbing moment of Adam Brent and of the memory of the way she had felt when she was in his arms. And further back, to the times in the glen, when they had walked and talked together and there had been a closeness between them that had been the start of her loving him.

Yes, anyone else would be second best. Jane was right, Mike wouldn't be satisfied with that. Kirsty hoped with all her heart that Jane was right in the other things she had just said about Mike—in her feeling that he would accept this better than Kirsty thought he would. Before he goes home, she told herself, I'll talk to him.

But before she could do this, Mike himself did the talking. A few days after Kirsty's talk to Jane, she went in to see him when she came off duty. He was in bed but she could see, from the wheelchair with his dressing-gown still on it, that he had been out.

'Taking the air?' she asked him, smiling.

'Yes,' he replied, 'Jane got permission to push me across to the park—pretty high living, after the confines of the hospital!' He looked at her. 'You could do with some fresh air yourself, Kirsty,' he told her. 'You've been working too hard.' Kirsty sat down in the chair beside his bed.

'Are you talking as a doctor?' she asked him lightly.

His blue eyes met hers levelly.

'No, I'm talking as your friend,' he said, his voice low. 'And while we're on that subject, there's something I'd like to say, Kirsty. I've really appreciated all you've done for me since the accident, and I've needed every bit of help and support. But things are different now, and I guess in more ways than one, it's time I began to learn to stand on my own feet.'

'Oh, Mike,' Kirsty began uncertainly, but he stopped her.

'Wait a minute,' he said. 'Let me get this off my chest. I honestly don't know what I would have done without you over this time, but you've got your life to live, and I've got mine. I hope we'll still see each other, and when I go into the annexe maybe you'll come and visit me, but—well, you know what I'm saying, Kirsty.'

Kirsty put out one hand, and he covered it with his, warm and reassuring.

'It's all right, you know, love,' he said gently. 'I mean that.'

'You've been talking to Jane,' Kirsty said, and it wasn't a question. He didn't deny this.

'Yes, I have,' he agreed. 'But she only put into words the things I've been thinking for quite some time. She helped me to get myself sorted out, that's all.' He smiled, and this time the smile reached his eyes. 'Quite a girl, is Jane. I had her in my book as a party girl and not much more, but that isn't true. And I really am glad that she helped me to get things out in the open. You should have spoken sooner, Kirsty.'

'I didn't want to hurt you,' Kirsty told him. His hand tightened on hers.

'It wasn't fair of me,' he said quietly. 'Because before the accident I was getting the message, if not loud and clear, fairly definitely, that you felt we were friends and nothing more. I just didn't want to hear that message, either then or after the accident. I kidded myself that everything was fine. You were coming to see me, you weren't going out with anyone else, and that was it.'

Jane was right, Kirsty thought with humility. She said I was making a mistake letting Mike think that. And for the first time the surprising thought came to her that, in fact, Jane seemed to be a better judge of Mike's reactions than she had been.

'Anyway,' Mike said clearly, 'we know where we stand now. It's great, Kirsty. I can say that now, without feeling I want to turn my face to the wall.' He smiled and his blue eyes were clear. 'You're not to worry about me! My heart is dented, maybe, but not broken. Plenty of pretty nurses at the annexe, I hear, and never mind the girls at home my mother will have lined up to come and see me.' That was another thing.

'Your mother,' Kirsty began with difficulty.

'I know,' Mike replied. 'And that's another thing you're not to worry about. My mother and father won't think you've let me down, Kirsty—they'll understand how things are.'

They will understand, Kirsty thought with sadness, but Adam doesn't. He thinks the worst of me and nothing is going to change that.

But that was her problem and not Mike's. She stood up and then bent down to kiss his cheek.

'Thanks, Mike,' she said softly. 'Thanks for everything.'

In a way, she thought later, that was her true goodbye to Mike, for when he left to go home by ambulance there was a big crowd of the hospital staff there to see him off. Kirsty kissed him, Jane kissed him and even Sister Dawson kissed him!

But when she turned to go back into the hospital, when the ambulance had driven away, Kirsty saw Adam Brent standing in the background, unsmiling, his eyes on her.

For a moment she faltered as she walked along. And then, with determination, she turned back to Jane and began talking, with an enthusiasm that she hoped didn't seem as forced as it was, of the party she had agreed to go to with Jane that night.

'You must,' Jane had told her firmly. 'You've got to start getting into circulation again, Kirsty.'

But it wasn't a success. I'm not the party kind of girl, Kirsty thought a little ruefully that evening, standing in the noisy and crowded room wishing she was anywhere else. Not like Helen Conway.

The girl who was engaged to Adam was once again having a marvellous time, but not with Adam. Her companion was the same young doctor she had been with before. Steve Hartley. Most of the time the two of of them were together, dancing, talking, laughing, and Kirsty thought that perhaps they were better suited than Helen and Adam. Although who was she to judge? she asked herself with some bitterness. She seemed to know so little about Adam Brent, and he about her, that he could think all the things he did about her.

After that Kirsty told Jane, politely but firmly, that she didn't want to go to any more parties. 'We're pretty busy on Harding,' she said, and that was true. 'I'm really only too pleased to come back to the flat, have a nice hot bath and put my feet up after a day at work.'

But somehow, as the days went by, she found she didn't seem to be able to relax when she came off duty. She would reach the flat feeling exhausted— sometimes too tired to go down to the dining-room for a meal—and although she would often go to bed early, she rose the next morning still feeling tired and unrefreshed.

They were short-staffed and each succeeding operation day became more and more pressured. Kirsty found herself hurrying from patient to patient giving pre-meds, preparing them both physically and mentally for their operations, often taking them down to theatre. And then she had to bring them back when they were ready and fit in post-operative care while she still had other patients going for their operations.

One operating day a few weeks after Mike left the hospital, she had just taken the last patient to theatre and hurried back to the ward when she was told that Sister Dawson wanted to see her. Sister Dawson was sitting at her desk in the duty room and Kirsty's heart turned over, for the older woman looked unusually serious.

'Is something wrong, Sister?' she asked quickly.

'Yes, Nurse Macrae, it is,' Sister Dawson returned.

Frantically, Kirsty's mind whirled from patient to patient. Had she slipped up on something, forgotten an injection or left a dressing unchanged?

'My work—' she began uncertainly, but Sister Dawson shook her head.

'My dear, there is nothing wrong with your work,' she said, and now she smiled. 'Except that you're doing too much. I know, we've been short-staffed, and it's been hard on all of us, but you are exceptionally conscientious, Nurse Macrae, and you've been pushing yourself too hard. And I think you have been under considerable strain as well, after young Dr Wilson's accident.'

Kirsty lifted her head high. 'I can manage, Sister Dawson,' she said, distressed. 'Really, I'm fine.' But there was no stopping Sister Dawson.

'I've arranged for you to have a check-up at the nurses' home, Nurse Macrae,' she said. 'We'll talk again after that.'

She had arranged for it to be done that very day, and a few hours later Kirsty, somewhat shaken, was told very firmly that she was to go and see Matron.

Apart from seeing Matron on her rounds, Kirsty had had very little to do with her. But she found that Matron seated in her office was less intimidating than Matron doing a ward round. In fact, Kirsty thought, surprised, she looks much younger than I'd imagined her to be.

'I have your medical report here, Nurse Macrae,' Matron said. And then, kindly, 'My dear, Sister Dawson is right. You've been over-working. I know you're not really due for any leave yet, but we're going to give you a fortnight and you're to go back to that beautiful glen you come from. I want you to sleep late, to get lots of fresh air and to eat well.'

'But Sister Dawson is so short-staffed!' Kirsty protested.

Matron shook her head.

'You will do Sister Dawson no kindness if you make yourself really ill,' she said firmly. 'And that is where you're heading.' She picked up a detailed list and studied it for a moment. 'I've arranged for Sister Dawson to have another staff nurse and a third-year student nurse as well. When you come back, come and see me and we'll talk about where you will work next.'

Kirsty left Matron's office in a daze, and when she got to the nurses' home she found that Home Sister had already booked her place on the overnight train. Jane and Andrea helped her to pack, and it was only when she was actually in the train that the reality of what was happening caught up with her.

I'm going home, she thought. Home to Invertorridon.

There was a slow, rising tide of happiness at the

thought of seeing her parents and her beloved glen, but at the same time she couldn't help remembering now how she had felt when she left the glen to come to the hospital. She had been so full of high hopes and dreams. Dreams of the work she was so looking forward to, and dreams of Adam Brent.

Now she was going back to the glen, and so much had changed. Too much, Kirsty thought sadly, would never be the same again.

CHAPTER ELEVEN

BUT THE glen itself hadn't changed. It was good to be home, there was no doubt in Kirsty's mind of that. It was only now that she was back that she realised that she had actually missed her mother fussing over her.

'And if the hospital meals are as grand as you've been telling me,' her mother asked her sternly, 'why is it that you've got so skinny, I would like to know!'

'I'm not skinny,' Kirsty protested, looking with dismay at the huge plate of porridge set in front of her at breakfast. But even as she protested, she had to admit that it was nice, in many ways, being treated as if she was a child, being told to eat up.

'She's fine, Morag,' her father said mildly. 'She's always been a wee thing, our Kirsty.'

'Och aye, a wee thing,' her mother agreed. 'But a healthy wee thing. Anyway, I'm right glad thon sister knew that the best thing to do with a lassie like this is to send her home to her mother.' She patted Kirsty's shoulder. 'Now, Kirsty, you'll just take the dogs and go out for a guid lang walk, and that will give you a fine appetite for your dinner.'

Obediently, because it was easier than trying to refuse, Kirsty managed to finish most of her plate of porridge. The dogs, eager at the sound of the word 'walk', were waiting for her, the old collie patiently, her nose on her paws, the young one sitting alert, his ears up.

'I've missed you, you know,' Kirsty told them, putting on the warm jacket her mother was holding out for her.

'Aye, you'll tell Jess and Rover that, but not a word of missing your father and me,' her mother said, and she smiled. 'Away you go, lass, and get the fresh air.'

Kirsty walked right to the head of the glen and along the burn, and up the lower slopes of Ben Cruach at the far end. Deliberately, she put all thoughts of anything and anyone else right out of her mind. The brown and gold of the glen in autumn was restful to her eyes and her mind, and there was a healing in the solitude. Just herself, and the dogs running ahead, she thought gratefully.

But there was a limit to the time she could keep at bay thoughts and memories of Adam Brent, for the two of them had walked along this very path together. And just here, Kirsty remembered, with a tightness in her throat, we sat, the two of us, and Adam talked about the hospital. And I listened to him and thought what a grand thing it would be to go and work there, and to see him.

'Do you ever see anything of that nice Adam Brent?' her mother asked later that day.

Kirsty had been half expecting the question, and she was able to answer lightly and easily.

'Yes, I've seen a bit of him,' she said casually. 'You must realise, of course, Mum, he's a junior surgical registrar and I'm just a staff nurse. But yes, I've seen him.' She bent down and patted old Jess, lying at her feet. 'He's engaged to one of the sisters at the hospital,' she said, not looking at her mother. 'A very pretty girl called Helen Conway.'

'That's nice,' her mother replied, and Kirsty was glad that her attention was on the potatoes she was peeling. 'I like to hear of a nice hospital romance.' She turned round. 'And what about this puir young man, Kirsty, this friend of yours? Is it true that he's to be able to walk again?'

'Yes, he is,' Kirsty said. 'For a while it looked as if he would be in a wheelchair, but Adam Brent— he was looking after Mike—got Cameron from Edinburgh to come and see him, and he tried a new technique that has just been developed for spinal injuries. And Mike is going to be all right.'

Her mother nodded. 'Aye, there's nothing like a Scottish doctor,' she said with satisfaction. 'I'm real glad to hear the young fellow is to be all right.'

A few days later—Kirsty began to lose track of the days, here in the autumn peace of the glens— there was a letter from Mike, sent on from the hospital. It was a bright, cheerful letter, and it warmed Kirsty's heart to read it. Mike said he was sorry to hear she hadn't been well, Jane had told him when she came down for the weekend. His mother and Jane had got on very well together, he said, once his mother managed to find out that Jane's beautiful russet hair was naturally that colour.

'I'll be at the annexe by the time you get back,' he

finished. 'Bet those tough physios will make me work hard! Come and see me sometime, Kirsty. Love, Mike.'

Kirsty folded the letter and put it back in its envelope, thinking, with some surprise, that Jane really had been right about Mike. It was a humbling thought, Kirsty told herself with some amusement, that she had been thinking that Mike depended so much on her, while in fact he was, as Jane had said, tougher than she had expected. But perhaps I was right, she thought, remembering. Perhaps, just at the start, he really did need me around.

Jane spending a weekend with Mike and his parents! She smiled. And Mike taking the trouble to mention that Jane and his mother had got on well together! I wonder . . .

Somehow, the cheerful letter from Mike gave her even more peace of mind and slowly, over the next day or two, she felt the strain and the tension of the last few weeks leave her, until she found that she had reached the stage where she could say to herself—all right, it's a pity that Adam Brent has let himself believe so badly of me, and it hurts that he has such a low opinion of me, a man I respect so much as a doctor. But I'm not going to let it get me down. When I go back to the hospital I will ask to work on some other ward where I need not see anything of him at all, and then I will just look on it all as part of growing up. And that will be just fine.

With that decided and behind her, Kirsty found that she could relax and allow the peace and the solitude of the glen, added to the warmth and the love of her parents, work their healing. Before she had been home for a week she knew that she looked and felt a different person.

She was sitting in the kitchen one afternoon, putting on her stout shoes ready to go out for a walk with the dogs, when she heard someone at the door and her mother answering it. A moment or two later the kitchen door opened and her mother came in.

'Kirsty,' she said, and Kirsty looked up at the surprise in her mother's voice, 'here's a visitor for you.'

Adam Brent stood behind her.

'Hello, Kirsty,' he said, quietly, his eyes on her face. 'How are you?'

'I'm all right,' Kirsty replied, unable to hide her own surprise.

'I heard from Sister Dawson that you were heading for a breakdown if you didn't let up,' Adam said, a little awkwardly. 'But I must say you look better than I had expected you to.'

And Kirsty was suddenly all too conscious of the freckles brought out by the autumn sunshine, of her brown hair left carelessly loose on her shoulders, of her old jeans and thick jersey.

'You should have seen her when she got here,' her mother put in. 'But Adam, what brings you here? I've been hearing from Kirsty how well you're doing down in London.'

Adam's eyes were still on Kirsty's face.

'I had a bit of leave due to me,' he said, 'and Dr Fraser said that he'd be glad to have me come to help out, any time I could. So I came. And since I'd heard that you weren't well, Kirsty, I thought I'd come right away and see how you were.'

'She was just off for a walk with the dogs, Adam,' Kirsty's mother said. 'Why don't you go too? You look as if you're needing some good fresh glen air yourself—and when the two of you get back, I'll have some scones ready. Now, off you go.'

'I'm sure Adam doesn't want—' Kirsty began.

'I'll enjoy that, Mrs Macrae,' Adam said firmly, at the same time.

And so a few moments later Kirsty found herself, still rather dazed, walking along the farm road with Adam Brent beside her. The whole thing seemed quite unbelievable! She didn't know what to say, so she said nothing.

'I was worried about you, Kirsty,' Adam Brent said, abruptly and surprisingly. 'Sister Dawson was really concerned.' He looked down at her. 'I didn't expect to see you looking so well.' Kirsty felt her face grow warm.

'It's being in the glen,' she said quickly, not looking at him. 'My mother feeds me too well and insists on me having lots of fresh air and exercise and early nights. I suppose that's why I'm so much better.'

They had reached the old stone bridge over the burn, and Adam stopped.

'Kirsty,' he said quietly. 'There's something I have to say to you. I went to Mike Wilson's home, to check up on him and to make arrangements for his treatment in the annexe, and we had a long talk.

He put me right on quite a few things. It seems I got the wrong picture, Kirsty. I don't know what to say, other than that I'm sorry. I should have known that you weren't the kind of girl to let someone down when you loved him.' He looked straight ahead. 'And Mike tells me that you never did give him any reason to think that you were in love with him. He says you were there when he needed you and it was only his selfishness that stopped him from admitting that, to himself and to you. I'm sorry, Kirsty.'

'It doesn't matter,' Kirsty said with some difficulty after a moment.

'It matters to me,' Adam said, his voice low. 'Kirsty—'

His hand was on her arm, and now the dream-like sense of unreality had gone. He was right here beside her in the glen, and suddenly it was almost more than she could bear.

'How is Helen?' she asked brightly. 'She suggested I might join the theatre team—I could do with a change from surgical.' Adam's hand dropped.

'Helen is very well,' he told her levelly. 'In fact, happier than she has been for some time. We're not engaged any longer, Kirsty.'

Kirsty remembered the laughter on Helen Conway's lovely face as she danced with Steve Hartley.

'I'm sorry, Adam,' she said, meaning it. His dark eyes looked down into hers.

'I don't know whether you'll believe me or not,'

he said quietly, 'but our engagement was broken by mutual consent. We both knew it wasn't going to work. Actually, I think we've known for some time, both of us. I certainly have.' He shrugged. 'It was a mistake from the start, but it took us some time to admit it. Anyway, Helen is now much happier, and so am I.'

Again, Kirsty was at a loss for words. Why was Adam Brent standing here beside her in the glen, explaining to her that he and Helen Conway were no longer engaged? Why was he looking at her like that, his eyes dark and fixed on her face, and waiting? What was he waiting for?

'I'm not putting any of this very well,' Adam said after a moment. 'I don't know why, Kirsty, but where you're concerned I don't seem to be able to see straight. I don't know why I was so blind when we were together here in the glen last year. I should have known—'

Kirsty wanted him to say it, to spell out for her just what he should have known. But at the same time she wanted him to stop, to go slowly.

'Kirsty,' Adam said, and then, unsteadily, 'come here.'

Kirsty stood still, making no move towards him. For a long time, it seemed to her, Adam Brent stood waiting. Then he took her in his arms fiercely, possessively, as if he could no longer hold himself back. His lips were warm on hers as he crushed her to him, and Kirsty felt her blood leaping in response.

It was a long time before he let her go, and when

he did, he looked down at her, his lips against her forehead.

'We have both been blind, you and I, Kirsty, my love,' he murmured. 'But that's all over, isn't it?'

Carefully, Kirsty moved back from him, knowing that she needed even this much distance to try to recover.

'I don't quite know what you're saying, Adam,' she said, after a moment. He smiled.

'I'm saying that I love you, Kirsty, and I hope— no, I *think*—that perhaps you love me too.'

Kirsty's heart had stopped its uneven thudding and settled to a steady rhythm again. But the warmth of his kiss was still there on her lips. If she didn't say this now, she could never say it—and she knew that it had to be said.

'Adam,' she began with difficulty, 'if you really loved me, how could you have believed the things you did about me? How could you have thought that I would walk out on Mike because he was to be in a wheelchair? And even before that. You knew me, you had known me here in the glen. You should have known that I wasn't—wasn't fast, and loose, and—and all the things you obviously thought I was.'

She didn't know that she was crying until Adam took out his handkerchief and dried her eyes. The gentleness of his touch was almost her undoing, but she forced herself to move away from him.

'Kirsty, love,' he said, taken aback, 'I've told you—I just haven't been able to see straight where you're concerned. Of course I should have known, but I wasn't being reasonable or logical, I was just reacting.'

His hands were on her shoulders, and he tilted her chin so that she had to look up at him.

'You hurt me, Adam,' she said, her voice low. 'I don't think you know just how much you hurt me.'

His lean brown face tightened. 'I do know, Kirsty, and I'll never forgive myself for that. But you're not going to hold that against me, are you?'

She turned her head away from him. Her own feelings were so strange and so confused that it wasn't going to be easy to make him understand.

'It isn't a case of holding it against you, Adam,' she said quietly. 'It's just—you have hurt me so much, I don't know how I feel about you any more.'

'How can you say you don't know how you feel about me, Kirsty? I know well enough how I feel about you, and I don't think I'm wrong about the way you feel.' His voice was uneven.

Unexpectedly, he kissed her again, a kiss that was hard and demanding, a kiss that left her breathless. Then, for a moment, his lips left hers.

'Kirsty, my love, my girl,' he murmured.

And this time his kiss was gentle and as tender and as loving as she could ever have wished. But still, when he released her, she was troubled.

'Can you still say you don't know how you feel about me?' he asked her.

She looked at him.

'Adam, I'm worried that maybe this is just a—a physical reaction. I admit that I feel . . . I like it when you kiss me, but—oh, Adam, I'm so mixed up about it all.'

He drew back from her. 'I've hurt you so much, Kirsty,' he said with sadness. 'I want to spend the rest of my life making up for that. Are you going to let me do that?'

'I don't know,' Kirsty whispered. 'I—I need time.'

'I'll wait,' Adam said quietly.

All Kirsty could do was look at him, and all she could feel was bewilderment and uncertainty.

CHAPTER TWELVE

KIRSTY WAS grateful, that day and the following days, that her mother asked no questions.

The strained atmosphere between she and Adam must have been all too obvious, particularly that first day. But her mother, after one swift glance at Kirsty's face, made tea for them and sat them both down at the big scrubbed kitchen table. Mrs Macrae asked Adam about his work and listened with interest as he told her how much he had learned in his time as junior surgical registrar at St Luke's.

'But the time in the glen will be doing you good, I'm sure,' she said comfortably when Adam was silent. 'You'll be tired, no doubt, and of course the London air is nothing like the glen air. Kirsty looked terrible when she got here, but she's just about her own self again.'

For a moment Adam's eyes met Kirsty's and she could hardly bear the questioning in them.

'I'd better go,' he said after a moment, standing up. 'I am here to give Dr Fraser some help, after all, and I told him I'd be back for evening surgery.' He smiled at Kirsty's mother. 'Mrs Macrae, your scones are just as good as I remembered them— thank you.'

'Och well, it's fine to see you back again, Adam,'

Mrs Macrae said, pleased. 'We'll be seeing you again, surely, while you're here?'

Kirsty wondered if her mother noticed the momentary hesitation before Adam steadily replied that he certainly hoped so.

'Kirsty, you go and see Adam out—I'll just clear away these things,' Mrs Macrae said, taking the cups over to the sink.

Neither of them saying anything, Kirsty and Adam went out of the kitchen door and round to where Dr Fraser's old car was parked. It was only when they had reached the car that Adam spoke.

'Will you allow me to come and see you, Kirsty?' he asked quietly.

His lean brown face was very still as he looked down at her, apart from a muscle that twitched in one cheek.

'I told you I would wait,' he said with some difficulty. 'And I told you that I wanted to spend the rest of my life making up for the way I've hurt you. But I'll play fair, Kirsty. I won't rush you and I won't touch you. If you think that what there is between the two of us is nothing but physical attraction, I won't try to cloud your judgment or confuse your thinking.'

His eyes were very dark as he looked down at her. 'I don't think that's true. I think that what I feel for you and you feel for me goes far beyond that. But I know that you have to come to that realisation for yourself. May I come and see you, Kirsty, whenever I can?'

If he hadn't come, Kirsty thought, I could have

gone on believing that it didn't matter to me what he thought of me, or whether I ever saw him again. But he's here beside me now, here in the glen, and I cannot pretend that he is nothing to me. At the same time, I don't know if I can ever forget how much he has hurt me, I don't know if I can ever put that behind me. And perhaps it would be better for both Adam and me if I just said no, here and now.

'Kirsty?' Adam said quietly.

'All right,' Kirsty replied after a moment. And then, because in spite of the way she was holding him off, she wanted to hear it, she asked him, 'Adam, did you really come to the glen to—to help Dr Fraser?'

His jaw relaxed. 'I came because I was worried about you and because I wanted to sort things out, Kirsty,' he told her, his eyes steady as he looked down at her. 'Of course, I'll be helping Dr Fraser while I'm here. It was true, he did say to me that any time I felt like coming back to Invertorridon he would be glad of some help. But I came to the glen because of you, Kirsty.'

When he had driven off down the farm road, Kirsty went slowly back inside and helped her mother to dry up the dishes and clear the table. And she thought, with love and gratitude, that her mother was a very understanding and accepting woman. Questions about Adam would have been more than she could have taken.

The following day she was determined that she would not sit around the house wondering if Adam would come to see her, wondering if he had really meant all that he had said. So she went off into the hills with the dogs, walking further than she had meant to, until she was breathless and tired and her muscles were aching pleasantly. From the top of the hill she had climbed she could see the countryside for miles, and she sat with her back to a tree, looking at the little town of Invertorridon in the distance. There was the hospital on the hill, and her own home, the fields spread out as if they were part of a toy farm.

Perhaps I should never have left here, she thought. Perhaps it would have been better if I had stayed in the glen and never gone to London, never seen Adam again. Then I would have been able to keep the memory of the time we had here together, untouched, and unspoiled.

But where was the point in thinking that way? she had gone, and she had met Adam again, and instead of remaining a dream, a man she scarcely knew, he had become all too real as they worked together at the hospital. And she had loved him and been hurt by him. There is no sense in pretending that none of that happened, Kirsty told herself firmly, for it did, and there is no changing it. Since there is no going back, one way or the other, I will have to be going forward.

Just how she was to go forward, she didn't yet know, but somehow there was less pressure in that thought up here on the hillside. She closed her eyes, glad to be out of the wind on this side of the hill. She had no intention of sleeping but she did, and when she opened her eyes it didn't really surprise her to see Adam coming up the hillside towards her and the dogs running eagerly to meet him.

'How did you know where I was?' she asked him, a little brusquely because of the sudden treacherous delight at the sight of him. He smiled, but there was anxiety in his eyes.

'Your mother thought you would probably head in this direction,' he told her. 'She gave me your father's binoculars so that I could look for you, and she said that if I didn't see you, I would surely see the dogs. I stood on the bridge down there, and sure enough I saw you sitting here, under the tree.' He hesitated. Then, his voice carefully casual, he said, 'You seemed to be sitting very still, Kirsty. Were you deep in thought?'

'I fell asleep,' Kirsty told him honestly.

Now he made no attempt to hide the concern in his eyes.

'Are you sure you're all right?' he asked her. 'Sister Dawson said she was really worried about you, you looked so tired and strained.

Her heart turned over at his very real anxiety, but she reminded herself firmly that this same man was the one who had so easily believed the worst of her more than once.

'I'm fine thank you,' she said shortly. 'It's just the fresh air and the exercise that made me sleepy.'

She turned away and called to the dogs knowing that his eyes were still resting on her but refusing to turn back to him. After a moment he took two big apples from his pocket.

'Your mother said we would both be hungry on a cold day like this,' he said, lightly, and handed her one.

Then he sat down beside her and began to eat his own. Kirsty, after looking at him warily for a while, ate hers too. Adam didn't talk, but after a while she realised, with some surprise, that there was much less strain between them. They finished their apples and Adam laughed at the young collie's obvious appreciation of his share, the cores. And then he began to talk, lightly and casually, about Dr Fraser and his practice here, asking her questions about people she had known all her life. In spite of herself, Kirsty relaxed completely, and when they began to walk down the path again and Adam took her hand in his, she left it there.

But that was all. He did nothing more and when they reached the farm road he released it to point to a bird and to ask her what it was. And he made no attempt to recapture her hand again.

The next day he phoned and asked her if he could pick her up and take her into Invertorridon for lunch. Kirsty, still guarded, agreed.

It was a pleasant day, and she enjoyed herself more than she would have thought possible, taking Adam around the places she had known and loved all her life. The school she had gone to, the church, the hospital, the little tea-room where they had home-made pies for lunch—it was a strange and disturbing feeling, sharing all these with Adam.

But he seemed determined to stick by the promise he had made. A brief touch of the hand was the only physical contact between them. At the end of the day, when he took her back to the farm and drew up outside the kitchen door, Kirsty couldn't help remembering that other time when they had sat in a car together, and the whirl of passion and emotion that had almost overwhelmed them. Did Adam remember that time too, she wondered?

She looked up at him and saw, her heart turning over, that he certainly did remember. He was very close to her in the confined space of the car, and it would have been so easy, she knew, to have moved, to have gone into his arms. But she was afraid. Afraid of the way she knew she would feel the moment his lips touched hers. Afraid to trust herself to him.

'Thank you, Adam,' she said quickly. 'I enjoyed lunch and I enjoyed having a look at Invertorridon through someone else's eyes.'

She knew that she hadn't imagined the shadow of disappointment in his eyes. But after a moment he smiled.

'I enjoyed it too, Kirsty. I'm going to be busy for the next couple of days—Dr Fraser has some work lined up for me at the hospital. I'll give you a ring.'

It was absurd and ridiculous, Kirsty told herself firmly, to feel just a wee bit disappointed, for was this not the way she wanted things?

She spent the next two days taking the dogs for long walks and doing some necessary thinking about what she was to do when she went back to the hospital. Before she left, she had spoken to Sister Dawson about the possibility of having a change from the ward. They both felt that it would benefit her to get some theatre experience, and Kirsty herself had always felt that she would enjoy being part of the theatre team.

But with Adam doing more and more operating it would mean that she would be seeing plenty of him, and she didn't know whether that would be a good idea. Or, she thought with honesty, whether it would be fair to him or to herself.

She was glad when Adam himself asked her what she thought of doing when he appeared at the farm a few days later and joined her at the kitchen fire. She had been sitting reading, for it was too cold and wet to go out.

'You did say you'd probably have a change,' he said, drinking the tea her mother had insisted on making for them before hurrying out to visit a neighbour who was ill. 'I know Matron likes you girls to get as much and as varied experience as possible. Have you thought about working in theatre for a while? I think you'd fit in well with the team.'

'Yes, I think I would like to work in theatre,' Kirsty said slowly. 'Sister Dawson said she'd speak to Matron about it if I wanted to, but—'

Adam looked down at her, his eyes questioning, and to Kirsty's annoyance she felt her cheeks grow warm.

'For goodness' sake, Kirsty,' he said impatiently, 'surely you know that you don't need to let any problems between you and me affect your work in the hospital? I can tell you without any doubt that when I'm working, as long as my theatre staff do everything they're supposed to do at the right time and in the right way, I couldn't care less about any personal connection I might have or might not have with any of them.' He hesitated, but only for a moment, before he continued telling her that it had never affected his working relationship when he had been engaged to Helen Conway, and it wouldn't, even now the engagement was now broken.

'I didn't really think it would make any difference,' Kirsty said quickly and not entirely truthfully. 'I just didn't want it to be awkward at all.' Adam stood up.

'I don't see why it should be,' he told her briskly. 'Kirsty, I'm going back to London at the weekend. I wondered if we might travel together?'

Kirsty shook her head. 'My ticket is booked for Tuesday,' she said.

'You could change it,' Adam suggested. And then, when she didn't say anything, he shrugged. 'As you wish, of course.'

The cool, casual tone of his voice made Kirsty all at once conscious of a tight ache in her throat, and she turned away quickly. But not quickly enough.

'Kirsty,' Adam whispered, and the sudden disconcerting gentleness brought a treacherous prickle of tears to her eyes. He took both her hands in his and she made no attempt to draw back, for she couldn't. She thought afterwards, in the days and weeks that followed, when they were both far away from the glen, that perhaps if he had taken her in his arms then . . . But he didn't take her in his arms. He held both her hands in his and looked down at her. 'You were right, my dear,' he said, his voice low. 'We do need time—both of us.'

She didn't see him again before he left the glen, although he phoned to say goodbye.

'See you at the hospital,' he said lightly. 'Do think about working in theatre, Kirsty.'

'I will,' she replied, protected by the anonymity of the telephone. 'Goodbye, Adam.'

Slowly, she put the receiver down, and once again she reminded herself that this was how she wanted things to be between them.

It was a strange feeling, going back to the hospital with so many things changed from her first coming there, when she had been so new, so hopeful, so full of dreams of the work she would do and of seeing Adam. Now it was all very different, Kirsty thought a little bleakly, as she greeted the porter and walked across to the nurses's home. She knew the hospital and she knew many of the people she would be working with.

Although she felt a little apprehension at the thought of doing different work, somehow the time she had spent at St Luke's had increased her confidence in herself as a nurse, so that she knew, really knew, that she could cope with the demands of being part of the theatre team—for she had decided that this was what she wanted to do. But the young and eager and hopeful Kirsty who had come here all those months ago had gone, to be replaced by one who was a little more realistic, and very much less certain that everything would work out happily and well.

Her room-mates welcomed her back with such pleasure that her fleeting feelings of depression lifted. Both Jane and Andrea were so genuinely delighted to have her back and to help her to catch up with hospital news, that in some ways Kirsty felt she had hardly been away.

And in spite of having told herself that it would happen, she was glad that she was busy unpacking when Jane, sitting cross-legged on Kirsty's bed, said casually, 'You won't know, of course, that the big romance is off?'

'The big romance?' Kirsty repeated casually, putting her sweaters neatly in her wardrobe.

'Adam and Helen,' Jane said. 'We all knew she was two-timing him, of course, and we thought there would be a big explosion when he found out, but it all rather fizzled out instead. They both seem quite happy that their engagement is broken. She's with Steve Hartley most of the time. I hear they're moving in together. And my friend Carol, who works in theatre, said she and Adam seemed to work together as well as ever. Of course, Adam's been away for a bit, I believe.'

For a moment, Kirsty's hands were still on the pile of neatly-folded clothes and she wondered if she should tell Jane that Adam had been in the glen—that she had seen him, spent time with him. But somehow she knew that she would be unable to say his name and speak about him lightly and easily, and Jane was quick and perceptive. So she said nothing, feeling fairly sure that Adam himself would not be likely to talk about where he had been.

'What about Mike?' she asked, deliberately changing the subject. 'I had a letter from him—he seems to be making progress.'

'He is,' Jane said warmly. 'You know, Kirsty, I always did think Mike was lots of fun, a great guy for a party, but there's a lot more to him, you know.' She frowned so fiercely, obviously expecting opposition, that Kirsty couldn't help smiling.

'I'm sure you're right, Jane,' she agreed. 'I certainly feel that he's shown a lot of courage in the way he's taken things since his accident.'

'I spent a weekend with him and his folks in Cornwall,' Jane said, her voice light and casual, but her cheeks glowing with heightened colour. 'Gave Mike a bit of company—he says he gets a bit lonely down there.'

Kirsty sat down on the chair and smiled at her friend.

'He told me you'd been,' she said quietly. 'And he said his mother seemed to get on very well with you once she'd found out that your hair is that colour naturally.'

Jane flicked a strand of her red-gold hair back from her face and smiled, too.

'She was a bit stand-offish at first,' she agreed. And then she said, 'You haven't changed your mind about Mike, have you, Kirsty? I mean, you don't feel sort of warmer towards him, maybe?'

This was very important to Jane, Kirsty saw.

'We'll always be good friends,' she said slowly. 'I really mean that, Jane. I'll always look on Mike as such a good friend. But nothing more. And I'm sure he sees it like that, too, now.' Jane's eyes were shadowed.

'I'd like to think that,' she said honestly, 'but I'm not so sure. You're pretty special to Mike, Kirsty.'

'I get the feeling from Mike's letters that you're becoming very special indeed to him, Jane,'

Jane uncoiled her long, slim brown legs. 'Maybe, maybe not,' she replied lightly, and the moment of closeness was over. 'We'll see, won't we?'

There was no problem about Kirsty's decision to work in theatre. She had phoned from the glen a few days before to talk to Sister Dawson, and when she had finished her unpacking she went down to study the duty lists and found that she was to start on theatre the next morning.

When she had finished breakfast and was hurrying along the passage that connected the nurses' home to the hospital she wondered, with some apprehension, what Helen Conway's attitude to her would be. It was with considerable relief that she found that Adam's ex-fiancée was treating her completely professionally and with no hint of strain or hostility in her manner.

'Nice to have you with us, Nurse Macrae,' she said. 'Now, I'll spend some time with you later today, but we're going right into an emergency appendicectomy, so I want you scrubbed up. Stick close to Nurse Carter, but don't get in anyone's way, and just get the feel of how we work as a team.'

Even the smallest green theatre-gown was a little big for Kirsty, but she tied it securely, put on her mask and her green theatre cap, and scrubbed up. Then, backing through the door with her sterile hands kept clear, she followed the rest of the nurses into the theatre.

Right away, she was impressed by the smoothness and the efficiency Helen Conway had achieved with her team of nurses. Each one seemed to know exactly what was expected of her at any given moment, as they completed the preparations for the operation.

The anaesthetist was already seated beside the unconscious patient, his eyes steadily on the instruments that told him of the stability of the patient's condition. The whole theatre team was ready when Adam Brent came in, gowned and masked, his sterile hands also held high, protected by the scrubbed rubber gloves.

'Morning, Sister Conway,' he said professionally. 'Everything all right, Jack?'

The anaesthetist nodded and Adam took up his position. For a moment, above the green mask, his eyes met Kirsty's and he gave, she thought, a small nod of recognition. And then Adam Brent the man was gone, and there was only Adam Brent the surgeon, working with the care and the skill that Kirsty had until now only heard about, to save a man's life.

CHAPTER THIRTEEN

AT FIRST, it seemed to Kirsty that she would never be sure enough and swift enough to be a worthwhile part of the theatre team, but within a few days she found that she was beginning to know what was expected of her. After that, as her confidence and her knowledge increased, she could get to know the different surgeons and their ways of working. Soon she could see that the time would come when she could hope to be as efficient as Helen Conway.

The girl who had been Adam's fiancée was an excellent theatre sister, Kirsty had to admit that. Each surgeon had his own procedure, his own favourite instruments, and sometimes it seemed to Kirsty that Helen Conway knew, even before the surgeon did, what would be required. She always seemed to be ready as the surgeon's gloved hand reached out.

'Not really,' Helen said when Kirsty, a little diffidently, asked her if she did anticipate the right instruments. 'But the longer you work with each surgeon, the better you know what he's likely to need and the faster you move.' She looked at Kirsty appraisingly. 'Don't worry, you'll do. I can see that you're already getting each one sorted out in your mind. We're lucky just now, they're all fairly even-tempered. I've known surgeons who shouted at theatre nurses for the slightest thing. Then you get nervous and you might even drop the tray of sterilised instruments! I know—it's happened to me, and not so long ago, either.' She smiled. 'That's when Adam and I began to get to know each other. He was so kind and so sympathetic.'

It still surprised Kirsty to hear the other girl discuss Adam Brent as casually as she did. And to see the two of them work together in the theatre, easily, efficiently, smoothly. Adam was right, Kirsty had to admit, when he said that nothing personal interfered with a working relationship.

Sometimes, as she stood close to him in the theatre, handing instruments to him, standing ready to pass sterilised swabs, she thought that he didn't even realise that this was Kirsty, the girl he had held in his arms, the girl he had kissed so fiercely, so passionately. It was better that way, of course, she told herself hastily, for what he was doing was too important to be affected by any distraction. But at the same time she couldn't help wishing that he would at least acknowledge that he knew she was there.

Then one day, as she was going out of the theatre after cleaning up, Adam came through from the surgeons' changing-room, his mask off, his green theatre-gown half-untied.

'Hello, Kirsty,' he said and smiled down at her. 'I thought I'd manage to catch you now.'

Kirsty looked up at him, her eyes wide, her breath suddenly catching in her throat, for this was the first time they had spoken since leaving the glen. And it was only surprise, she told herself hastily, that was making her feel so breathless.

'Don't look so worried,' Adam said easily. 'I'm not going to bawl you out for anything. I think Helen would be furious if I did, she hates to have her nurses intimidated in any way. I just wanted to say you're doing fine, Kirsty. I always thought you were a good nurse, but it isn't everyone who has the makings of a good theatre nurse.'

'Thank you,' Kirsty murmured, a little taken aback, and carefully stopping herself from using his name, although he had used hers. 'I—I'm certainly enjoying working in theatre.'

'I'm glad to hear it,' Adam said. His voice was warm and his smile was pleasant, and she was pleased with what he had just said. So why, Kirsty wondered forlornly, do I feel just a wee bit disappointed?

'I'll give you a ring sometime,' Adam said easily, turning to go. 'We might go out for dinner or a show, if that's all right with you?'

'Thank you,' Kirsty said sedately, and the momentary disappointment was miraculously gone. 'I would like that fine.'

As Adam went out of the door, Helen Conway came through from the theatre.

'Was that Adam you were talking to?' she asked curiously, and Kirsty, to her own annoyance, felt her cheeks grow warm.

'Yes, it was,' she replied. 'He was just—just—'

There was amusement in the blonde nurse's blue eyes—amusement, and a thoughtful look.

'Of course, I'd forgotten that you and Adam are old friends, aren't you?' she asked.

'Och well, maybe in a way we are,' Kirsty replied quickly. Too quickly, she knew, as the amusement deepened in the older girl's eyes.

'Don't worry, Kirsty,' Helen said briskly. 'Adam and I together were a disaster, and we should both have admitted it much sooner than we did.'

'Oh, but he's not—I'm not—I mean, he was only—'

Kirsty stopped, not knowing what she really wanted to say. Helen Conway patted her shoulder.

'I'm sure he's not, and you're not, but I just wanted to tell you that,' she said. 'Are we finished in here? You'd better go off for lunch now. I want you back in time to check the theatre for the afternoon ops.'

Kirsty had been working in theatre for almost a month when she had a phone call just after she came off duty. Hurrying out of the flat to the nearest telephone in the corridor, her uniform still on, she wondered, in spite of herself, if it was Adam. But it wasn't Adam, it was Mike.

'Darling Kirsty, how are you?' he asked, and her heart lifted at the old exuberance in his voice. And without giving her a chance to reply, 'Listen, I've just checked with home sister and I know you're off this weekend, so what about just getting on the train and coming to Cornwall for a couple of days? It would do you the world of good. My folks would love to see you, and so would I. I've got the train times here and I think you could catch the 8.30.'

Five minutes later Kirsty, still breathless, found that she had agreed to spend the weekend in Cornwall with Mike and his parents.

'That should be very nice. I'm sure you'll enjoy it,' Jane said a little formally, when Kirsty went back to the flat.

Kirsty wanted to say something to take the polite coolness from Jane's clear blue eyes, but she didn't know what, so she said nothing. And Jane, after a moment, began to talk quickly, animatedly, about a lecture they were all supposed to go to, on civil defence.

'. . . And can't you just see us all gathering up our medical supplies and making for the nearest safe place, and Sister Dawson checking that our caps are on properly?'

'Jane,' Kirsty said, little desperately, 'Mike and I are just good friends, we both know that!'

'Of course you are,' Jane replied brightly. 'We're all good friends, aren't we?' Kirsty gave up then.

Just as she had to give up on the following night, when Adam Brent at last phoned to ask her to spend Friday evening with him and she had to explain that she was going to Cornwall for the weekend.

'That should be very nice for you,' Adam said after a moment, and the same careful politeness was in his voice. 'Have a lovely time, Kirsty.'

'Thank you, I will,' Kirsty replied, just as politely, and she knew that to Adam, she couldn't even say that she and Mike were just good friends.

Adam knew that himself, for not only had Kirsty told him, Mike had made it plain as well. And yet the reserve and the formality were there in his voice.

'I'm sorry,' she said, simply.

'That's all right,' Adam replied. 'Some other time, perhaps.'

'Perhaps,' she agreed, and when he said goodbye she put the receiver down. He said that he would give me time, she thought, bleakly, and he said that he wouldn't rush me, and he's certainly sticking to his word!

In many ways, she couldn't help feeling that it was a relief to leave the hospital behind her on Friday and get on the fast train to Cornwall, to sit with her eyes closed, almost asleep, lulled by the smooth motion that was taking her far away from St Luke's. And from Adam Brent.

To her surprise, Mike was at the station when the train reached Falmouth. He was on crutches now, but he was moving confidently and with agility and all the strain had gone from his face.

'Look, no hands,' he said triumphantly, as she reached him. He handed his crutches to his father and put his arms around her. 'Kirsty, it's good to see you!'

His eyes were clear and untroubled, and his arms around her warm and affectionate and nothing more. I was right, Kirsty thought happily. We really are good friends, Mike and I.

'It's good to see you,' she returned, meaning it with all her heart. She turned to Mike's father and greeted him. 'Hello, Mr Wilson, it's so nice of you to have me here for the weekend.'

'You girls work hard, you need a break,' Mr Wilson replied, as he handed Mike back his crutches. 'And besides, this son of mine is impossible if he has to do without female company.'

'I can well believe that,' Kirsty agreed, and she turned with the two men to go out of the station. 'Mike, you really are coming on well.'

'Give me another few weeks and I'll be finding out how soon I can get back to work,' Mike said, and he smiled. 'Then I'll have all the female company I want! I bet all you girls are missing me, Kirsty.'

'Of course we are,' Kirsty agreed. 'St Luke's isn't the same without you, Mike.'

Mike's mother greeted her affectionately and took her to her room, telling Mike firmly that Kirsty must be tired, there would be time enough for talking in the morning. Kirsty, who had been just a little worried about Mrs Wilson's reaction, for she'd obviously been thought of as Mike's girlfriend at the time of the accident, realised with relief that he must have been able to make his parents understand how things really were between the two of them. She slept well that night, with the sound of the sea the last thing she was conscious of—and the first thing, when she woke.

'It's a bonny place, this,' she said to Mike later in the day, when they were sitting near the cliffs. They had been able to bring the car close enough for

Mike, on his crutches, to reach a seat set a little back, sheltered by a huge rock.

'But not as bonny as your glen?' he asked.

'Well, it's bonny in a different way,' Kirsty replied, smiling. 'Mike, I'm so glad to see how well you're coming on. Not only with your walking, but in yourself.'

'I was a bit of a misery for a while,' Mike agreed cheerfully. 'In fact, I must have been unbearable.'

'No, you weren't,' Kirsty told him, meaning it. 'You were very good for most of the time, just— sometimes, you were down.'

'Thanks for that, Kirsty,' he said, and he took both her hands in his. 'And thanks for all you did for me when I really needed you.'

She looked at him, a little troubled, but he smiled.

'It's all right,' he said. 'I mean that. I just had to be completely sure. I had to see you again and make certain I wasn't carrying any torches, or feeling that anyone but you would be second-best, before—'

Before what? Kirsty wondered. But she said nothing.

The rest of the weekend was pleasant and relaxed and, on the train again, she felt as if in some ways the short break had done her almost more good than her time in the glen. The weather had been good and the sun and the sea air had brought out a few freckles on her nose.

'You look as if you've been on a cruise. You're almost sunburnt!' Jane said when Kirsty passed on to her some flowers Mike's mother had sent.

'I feel as if I've had a really good break,' she
agreed. 'Seems as if I was away longer than just a
weekend.' She hesitated and then, not looking at
Jane, she said, 'It's always nice seeing people
you're fond of, and I'm really very fond of Mike. I
look on him as someone who'll always be a good
friend, and he feels the same way.'

For a moment, Jane's blue eyes held hers en-
quiringly. Kirsty didn't look away and although
neither of them said anything more, there was
something in the way Jane smiled that told Kirsty
that her friend believed what she had said.

Adam Brent didn't operate until the afternoon
the next day, and then it was a long and compli-
cated operation for a lung tumour. The chances of
removing the tumour successfully were not high,
and this knowledge brought an increased tension to
every member of the operating team. You could
almost, Kirsty thought, hear a small sigh of relief
from every single person when Adam said quietly,
'We've done it.'

Immediately the atmosphere in the theatre lightened and when the patient had been wheeled
through to the recovery room, Adam turned to
Helen Conway. 'Thanks, Helen,' he said. 'You and
your girls were terrific.'

'You weren't too bad yourself, Adam,' Helen
returned.

For a moment, as Adam walked out of the
theatre, his eyes met Kirsty's and she thought that
beneath his mask he smiled faintly. But all he was

saying, Kirsty reminded herself, was thanks for being part of the team. And isn't that all I'm wanting him to say? For now, at least?

That night he phoned her and asked, very casually, if he could take her out to dinner the following evening. Kirsty, proud of the casual sound of her own voice, thanked him and said she would like that.

'You look as if your weekend in Cornwall has done you good,' Adam said politely, when they were seated that evening in the little Italian restaurant he had chosen. 'How is Mike coming on?'

'Very well,' Kirsty told him. 'He manages fine with his crutches, and he can even stand without them. And,' she hesitated, but only for a moment, before she went on carefully, 'And I think he's a lot better in himself. He's much more positive, talking about getting back to work even.'

'I'm glad to hear that,' Adam said. He coughed. 'You must be relieved to see how much progress he's made, I'm sure.'

'Yes, I was,' Kirsty replied, a little puzzled.

'And glad to see him again,' Adam went on determinedly. And then, not looking at her, 'Perhaps you felt a little differently, seeing him again after all this time? No, Kirsty, I don't mean because he can walk again, because he's going to be all right. I just mean—you always used to look as if you were having such fun together, the two of you, so carefree, so . . .' His voice died away, and then he tried again. 'I thought perhaps you had really enjoyed meeting each other again.'

At last, realisation dawned on Kirsty. 'I told you before, Adam,' she said clearly, 'that Mike and I are good friends. I meant it then, and I mean it now.'

For a moment his eyes held hers, questioning. And then, almost as if he couldn't help himself, his hand covered hers on the table for one moment, fiercely, possessively. But before Kirsty could even begin to wonder how she felt, his hand had left hers and he was discussing the menu, asking her if she had tried Mario's tagliatelle. And the feeling and the moment had gone, as if they had never been.

They talked shop, discussing operations that had been done since Kirsty started in theatre, and then Adam told her about operations she had yet to see. His reserve left him. His dark eyes were alight, his lean brown face alive, as he talked of the work they both loved. They lingered over coffee for a long time, still talking, and it was late when they left the little restaurant and walked back towards the hospital and the nurses' home. Kirsty was glad, without allowing herself to dwell too long on her own feelings, that they had walked rather than coming in the car, for it was pleasant to dawdle back along the side-streets that would take them to the back door of the home. They chatted idly, Adam laughing sometimes at some comment Kirsty made about the people they worked with. But at last the gate was in sight and they both stopped.

'I have enjoyed myself, Adam,' Kirsty said, forgetting her decision to be a little cooler, a little more formal. 'It was a lovely evening.'

'I enjoyed it too, Kirsty,' Adam replied, looking down at her. 'We'll do it again.'

But even as he said it, in some strange, indefinable way there was once again the distance and the reserve between them. And now, after the closeness they had had, it was more than Kirsty could bear.

'Adam,' she said, her voice low, and she held out one hand to him. 'Adam, I wish . . .'

His eyes darkened. 'So do I, Kirsty, so do I,' he said tightly.

And then, with no warning, his arms were around her and his lips were hard on hers as he crushed her to him. Everything in Kirsty responded to him, and she clung to him. Until as suddenly as he had taken her in his arms, he let her go.

'I'm sorry, Kirsty,' he said, shakily. 'Don't make it too hard for me, if you want me to stick to the terms of the agreement. Goodnight.'

And he strode off into the night, a tall lean figure. But Kirsty's eyes were so blurred with tears that she could hardly see him. Slowly, she went upstairs. *The terms of the agreement*, he had said. It wasn't as businesslike as that, she thought sadly. It was just that I needed time, time to sort out my own feelings, time to let myself find out if I can ever really forget that Adam hurt me so much. Time to know if—if it could ever be all right again for us.

When she was in his arms there was that fierce and immediate response of her body to his, of her blood to his. She wondered if she was being foolish to deny this, foolish to ask for anything more than this. And yet as soon as he let her go she remembered all that there had been between them.

I don't know, she thought forlornly. I just don't know.

There was some comfort and some help in the demands of a fully-booked and short-staffed theatre over the next few days. Every one of the nurses was kept so busy that there was hardly a moment to think. And at the end of the day Kirsty was so tired that she was glad to go to bed early.

'And you still say you're enjoying being in theatre?' Jane asked at the end of the week, coming in to say goodbye to Kirsty.

'Yes, I am,' Kirsty returned, truthfully. 'I love it.'

'Better you than me,' her friend said.

'Have a lovely holiday, Jane,' Kirsty said then. 'You'll enjoy having longer in Cornwall than just a weekend.'

'Yes, I will,' Jane replied, turning to pick up her coat. 'I was quite pleased when Mike suggested it. His father says at least it's someone else for Mike to have a game of chess with!'

Kirsty shook her head, smiling, when Jane had gone. She was certain now of how Jane felt about Mike, but she knew that Jane didn't dare to let herself hope too much. Remembering some of the things Mike had said when she spent the weekend there, Kirsty thought that perhaps it wouldn't be too long before both Mike and Jane admitted their feelings.

It was in the middle of the week that she had a

phone call from Jane, a breathless, incoherent phone call that took her a few minutes to understand.

'And then,' Jane told her, 'Mike said every time he saw me, he missed me more and more when I went away, but he'd always thought I was just out for a good time, and so he didn't say anything. Until today! And now it's all right, and we're engaged, and we're having a party to announce it next Saturday, Kirsty, and you've got to come!'

'I suppose I have,' Kirsty agreed, laughing. 'What wonderful news, Jane! I'll check the trains and let you know.'

'Oh, you don't need to do that,' Jane told her. 'I've just phoned Adam Brent—Mike wants him there, too. He'll pick you up at 7.30 and bring you down.'

Slowly, Kirsty put the receiver down, not sure whether she felt pleased or dismayed at the prospect of driving down to Cornwall with Adam, considering the way they had parted.

CHAPTER FOURTEEN

In the following days, Kirsty wondered many times
how things would go as she and Adam travelled
together to Cornwall for the engagement party.
And she was glad that she had prepared herself, for
the reality was very much as she had imagined.

Adam was friendly, entertaining, even fairly
talkative, discussing possible wedding presents for
Mike and Jane, chatting about changes in the
theatre team. But he was also remote and obviously
polite Kirsty thought. He seemed determined to
keep her at arms' length, determined that he would
not again let his feelings show as they had the other
night.

And, of course, because that was how he was,
that was how Kirsty was as well. She raised her chin
determinedly, smiled at anything amusing he said,
gave him her opinion of useful and welcome presents for the newly-engaged couple, but kept it cool.

'Would you like to stop for something to eat?' he
asked her, half-way through the journey.

'No,' Kirsty said quickly, before she could stop
herself, remembering the two of them sitting at
the small candlelit table with the red and white
gingham cloth, and remembering that moment
when Adam's hand had covered hers. 'No, thank
you, Adam,' she said more politely. 'Not unless

you need something?'

'A quick cup of coffee and a sandwich will do me nicely,' Adam said.

They stopped at the next bypass and drew up to a service station, collected a tray, two cups of coffee and a plate of sandwiches and sat down at a small table. Nothing, Kirsty thought, could have been less like the intimate and warm atmosphere at Mario's the other night. For a moment, Adam's eyes met hers and she knew that he was thinking the same. But he said nothing about it, only remarked, with truth, that the coffee was even worse than the canteen coffee at the hospital.

After they reached Falmouth she had to direct him to Mike's parents' home. Although it was late, the house was blazing with welcoming lights and as soon as the car drew up, the door opened and Jane came hurrying out, her red-gold hair loose on her shoulders, her face glowing. Mike was immediately behind her, moving, Kirsty saw, even more easily on his crutches.

'You won't be needing these for much longer,' Adam said with a swift and professional glance.

'I plan on throwing them away before the wedding,' Mike replied, balancing himself on one crutch as he hugged Kirsty and then shook Adam's hand. 'No way am I going on my honeymoon on crutches!'

'I haven't noticed your crutches cramping your style too much, lover-boy,' his fiancée told him.

'Quiet, woman, you'll ruin my reputation as the

most respectable young doctor at St Luke's,' Mike told her.

Kirsty, her heart lifting, saw with joy that, beneath the teasing and the banter, the look Mike and Jane exchanged was warm and loving. They were so right for each other, she thought with complete certainty. She remembered now what Mike had said when she spent the weekend here, about having to see her again, to be sure, before . . . And she knew now that their meeting that weekend and confirmed for him what she had known, that there was a deep and lasting friendship between them, but that he could move on from there and admit to his growing love for Jane.

She saw Adam looking thoughtfully at the young nurse and doctor together, and she wondered if he, too, was seeing that she had been right, or if there were still doubts in his mind. But there was no chance for her to talk to him alone, then or through the following day, for she was busy helping Jane and Mike's mother to prepare food for the party to be held that night. Adam was kept busy moving furniture and driving to nearby Falmouth to collect things Mrs Wilson kept realising she needed.

Kirsty wore a new dress for the party, an Indian cotton dress of soft rose-pink, and she hesitated between wearing her hair loose on her shoulders or sweeping it up in a knot of curls. Without allowing herself to examine her own feelings too deeply, she knew that tonight she wanted to look completely different from the way she looked at work.

Which was why she had chosen the pink dress, instead of her usual favourite green—for she wore a green theatre-gown every day of her working life, with her hair neatly tucked out of sight inside the cap.

'Och, Kirsty, you're a foolish girl,' she told herself, admitting this as she looked into the mirror. She decided to compromise with her hair, lifting the curls high at the back, but leaving soft loose tendrils around her face.

And what is more, she thought with some severity, you will have to be making your mind up one way or the other about Adam Brent, for a man like him is not the kind to wait around indefinitely for a lassie to decide how she feels. And it is far from fair to him, the way things are.

She knew that she should either tell him that things would never be right between them and it was better for them to part, or she should tell him that she loved him, tell him that nothing that had happened in the past between them made any difference. But somehow she could do neither. Not yet. But she would have to before long, she knew that.

Because neither she nor Adam knew Mike's friends or the relatives who came to the party, it was inevitable that they should spend most of the evening together. Kirsty was glad that the party was a big, noisy one, with music playing most of the time, so that it was impossible to do much more than exchange a few words in between dancing and eating and drinking a toast to the newly-engaged couple.

'Speech, speech,' one of Mike's cousins shouted, and someone turned the music off as Mike stood up, leaning on one crutch, and with his other arm possessively around Jane's shoulders.

'I'm an action man, rather than a speech man,' Mike said, and to prove it he turned and kissed his fiancée with considerable enthusiasm and expertise. 'All I want to say is this—I reckon I'm the luckiest man in this room, and I want to thank you all for coming tonight to share in our happiness. Oh, and I'd specially like to thank Adam Brent and Kirsty Macrae for coming from St Luke's for the party. And thanks, Adam, for all you did for me at the time of the accident. Kirsty, thanks for everything.'

The music began again and Adam took Kirsty's glass from her fingers, stood up, and took her hand in his.

'I could have done without the honourable mention,' he murmured.

'So could I,' Kirsty agreed, and she wondered if he had felt as uncomfortable as she had, to have their names linked together as they had been.

It was well after midnight before the last guest left, and Kirsty and Jane and Mrs Wilson finished the washing-up while the men put the furniture back in order. They all had a cup of tea together in the kitchen before going to bed.

'Goodnight, Kirsty,' Adam said, at the top of the stairs. Fleetingly, he touched her cheek. 'You look tired—sleep well.'

Kirsty did sleep well, but it wasn't much wonder,

she thought when she woke the next morning, for it had been a long and busy day, not to mention the sea air that was so different from the London air she had grown accustomed to.

The rest of the household seemed to be asleep and she pulled on jeans and a thick jersey and went quietly downstairs and out into the garden that extended to the edge of the cliffs. In spite of her warm clothes, the early morning sea air was chilly, and she soon turned to go back into the house, to make some tea.

But Adam was coming across the lawn to her, and Kirsty knew, from the determined line of his jaw, that now there would be no escaping. She was going to have to make a decision, one way or the other.

But before Adam reached her, the telephone rang inside the house. After a moment's hesitation, he turned and went back inside to answer it. Kirsty followed him slowly. When she reached the hall, he had just put the receiver down, and she knew, by the shock on his face, that something had happened.

'There's been a train accident,' he told her tersely. 'At the level crossing just outside Falmouth. That was Mike's uncle on the phone, he's the local doctor. He hoped that we were still here—he needs all the help he can get. Will you wake Jane?'

Jane reacted, as did Kirsty and Adam, swiftly and professionally. She was ready in five minutes and made it quite plain to Mike that he would have to stay at home—for with his crutches there was very little he could do.

'And if someone hurrying past knocked into you, all the good of the operation could be undone, Mike,' Adam pointed out levelly. 'Look, as soon as we know what's happened we'll get a message to you. Maybe your uncle could use some help at the hospital.'

'Maybe he could,' Mike agreed, and Kirsty saw, with admiration, that he wasn't allowing his own frustration at his uselessness to hold them up. 'You'd better get on your way.'

Kirsty didn't know what she had expected but, in spite of her training, there was a moment of panic when she saw the two railway carriages lying on their side and the big transport lorry leaning drunkenly against them.

Adam hurried over and the two girls followed him to where Mike's uncle, Dr Wilson, was organising the first ambulance. The two doctors exchanged a few words and Adam turned back to Jane and Kirsty.

'No one killed,' he told them quietly, 'but some nasty injuries. We'll deal with what we can here, and we'll send the others up to the hospital. Do the best you can—Dr Wilson and I are here if you need us.'

Kirsty and Jane, after one quick glance at each other, rolled up their sleeves and got to work. There were a number of children who had been on the way to Sunday school in Falmouth, and although most of them were only bruised and shaken, there were grazes to be cleaned and bandaged and a few query fractures and sprains, including one small boy whose leg, Kirsty was sure, was broken.

'Just lie still,' she told the child. 'I'd like Dr Brent to have a look at your leg.'

She found an older child and left the little boy in his charge for a moment, while she went to see if Adam could come over.

'Yes, I think you're right,' he agreed, and he looked around, checking. 'We'll splint it to immobilise and I'd like him over here, ready for the ambulance to take. He'll have to be X-rayed. Hold that steady for me, Kirsty—good girl.'

When they had finished and the boy was lying on one of the seats that had been taken from the train, Kirsty went back to her cleaning and bandaging. Sometimes as she worked she looked across at Adam. His dark hair had fallen over his forehead and there was a streak of dirt down one cheek. Now that it was quieter, she could hear his voice as he talked to the shaken passengers, explaining and reassuring.

Once he looked up, and his eyes met hers. He smiled faintly and nodded. And Kirsty, strangely moved, went back to her own work. For a while she and Jane worked together, then Dr Wilson called Jane over to help him.

When the most pressing injuries had been dealt with, the doctor's wife, Mrs Wilson, came to Kirsty with a mug of steaming coffee.

'And here's one for Dr Brent too,' she said, briskly. 'I'm sure you both need it. You take this one to him.'

Kirsty straightened, realising for the first time that her back was aching. Adam had just finished putting splints on an injured arm when she reached him.

'Coffee, Adam,' she said to him.

'I'll get it later,' he said, without looking up.

'You'll have it right now,' Kirsty told him. 'You must be needing it.' He stood up, and took the mug from her.

'I always did think you could be pretty bossy, given the chance,' he said to her.

And there, among all the people they had cared for and tended and helped, with Adam's face streaked with dirt and her own probably not much better, Kirsty knew, with complete certainty, that it was all right. The barriers between them had gone as they worked here together. Adam was her man, the man she loved in every way, the only man in the world for her.

She was glad that he hadn't seen the way she was looking at him, that he had turned away, for this was no time for their own feelings—there was work to be done. But the most serious cases had all been taken to the hospital, and those with only minor injuries or shock were now being taken to the church hall.

Half an hour later, Kirsty and Adam finished cleaning up and bandaging the last patient, an old farmer with a jagged cut on his leg.

'I think that's about it, Kirsty,' Adam said wearily. 'I thought earlier we should move up to help at the hospital now, but Dr Wilson and Jane have gone up, and he sent a message to say they don't need us at the moment, so I suppose . . .'

He stopped. One of the helpers was coming towards them, holding by the hand a small girl whose arm they had bandaged earlier.

'Something more wrong with her?' Adam asked, but the woman shook her head.

'Not with Jenny here, but she says her brother Ian was with her, and we've just checked at the hospital and at the church hall, and no one has seen him. I thought he might still be with you, but I see you've no one here.'

Above the child's head, Adam's eyes met Kirsty's, and she knew that the same thought was in both their heads. Adam knelt down.

'Was Ian in the same carriage as you, Jenny?' he asked the child.

She nodded.

'He was with me,' she said tearfully, 'and then the lorry crashed into the train and I hurt my arm. And we all fell on the floor, and the window broke, and then one of the girls helped me to climb out, and—and I thought Ian would be coming too, but I don't know where he is.'

Adam stood up.

'Do you think you could show me which carriage you and Ian were in?' he asked.

'It's that one,' Jenny said, pointing, 'the one that's broken more than the other one. The seats are all broken inside. Even the floor's smashed up.'

The floor *was* mangled, and with the carriage on its side as it was, it was just possible that a child could have fallen through into the wreckage and no one had realised. But if that had happened, how badly hurt must he be? Kirsty wondered, sick at heart, for none of the rescuers had heard a sound.

'Take Jenny back to the church hall,' Adam said quietly. 'I think she needs a cup of tea and a biscuit. We'll find Ian! All right?'

The little girl looked at him for a moment. 'All right,' she agreed doubtfully.

Adam waited until the woman had taken her away and then he turned to Kirsty.

'If he is down there, he must be unconscious,' he said, and Kirsty knew that she hadn't imagined the momentary pause. He stretched flat on the tilted floor of the carriage and peered into the tangle of wreckage below. 'Ian! Ian, are you there?'

Kirsty, watching him, saw him stiffen.

'Listen, Kirsty,' he said urgently. 'Am I imagining it, or is there a sound?'

Kirsty balanced herself beside him and got her head as close to the hole as she could, while Adam called the boy's name again.

And now she heard it too—a faint moan, a sigh of pain or of distress.

'He's down there,' she said. 'Adam, when are they going to move the carriages?'

'I don't know,' Adam replied, slowly. 'Kirsty, I'm going to try to get down beside him. Maybe I could lift him out.'

But the gap was too small, and although Adam tried to enlarge it, there just wasn't enough room for him.

'I think I could get down,' Kirsty said, when he had to give up.

'No,' Adam said sharply, but Kirsty ignored him, and began to climb through. It was a tight squeeze but she was pretty sure she could make it.

'Hold on,' Adam said, when they both saw that she could do it. 'Don't go any further, Kirsty, until I see if I can get a torch. And I'll send someone for some equipment to move some of this.' He was back very quickly, with a torch.

'Got it from the cottage,' he told her briefly. 'And they've sent for the breakdown van, it might be able to do something.'

Kirsty edged herself down gingerly. In the wreckage it was very dark, and she was glad of the lamp Adam managed to pass to her. She had to crouch on all fours. 'Any sign of the boy?' Adam asked, his voice muffled.

'I don't think so,' she began, and then she stopped. The boy was there, in a small crumpled heap. She shone the torch on him and saw that he had a bad cut on his forehead and his eyes were closed. There wasn't even room for her to kneel beside him, but she checked swiftly and professionally, and found his pulse.

'Adam, he's here,' she said breathlessly. 'He's unconscious and he has a cut on his head, but his pulse doesn't seem too bad. I'm going to try to lift him up and hoist him up to you.' She had to find a place to wedge the torch while she tried to lift the boy.

'Careful, Kirsty,' Adam said quietly. 'I don't know how steady some of that mess down there is.'

I don't know either, Kirsty thought, and as she got the unconscious boy up into her arms—grateful that he wasn't much bigger than little Jenny—she felt the tilted carriage lurch. Slowly, steadily, with the boy in her arms, she inched backwards on her knees the way she had come down, knowing that this would be the most difficult part.

Adam had another torch, and he was shining it down the gap and making her task easier. From here, the hole looked so small that Kirsty wondered how she had managed to get down it.

'I can't get any further down,' Adam told her. 'If you can ease him just a little higher—the ambulance is standing by ready to take him to the hospital. Yes—I've almost got him.'

There was no further foothold. Kirsty stretched, and pushed, and then she felt the weight of the boy being taken from her. But at the same moment something moved under her and she felt herself lurch wildly. There was nothing she could do to stop herself falling, only one moment of breath-catching fear, and then her head hit something very hard and pain shot through her. She heard Adam's voice, agonised.

'Kirsty!' And then there was nothing.

A long time later—she heard how long afterwards—she opened her eyes and realised, slowly, that the room that was moving dizzily around her was a hospital room. When the dizziness receded a little and she turned her head to one side, she saw Adam. His eyes, dark and anxious, were fixed on her face. The one thing she needed to know more than anything else, was how the boy was. But when she tried to ask Adam, her voice seemed to be little more than a whisper.

'Ian?' Adam repeated. 'He's all right—concussed, and pretty badly grazed, but that's about it.' He smiled, but the anxiety was still in his eyes. 'I think you're about as badly concussed as he was, you've been out for ages. Mike and Jane have been here, and Mike's parents—I promised I'd let them know when you came round. I'll only be a moment.'

She closed her eyes when he went out of the room, and he came back so quietly that she didn't hear him until he sat down beside her and took her hand in his.

'Adam?' she murmured, and even to say his name was an effort, when all she wanted was to close her eyes. 'Don't go away—don't leave me.'

His hand tightened on hers.

'I won't,' he promised. Kirsty closed her eyes.

When she woke again, her head felt a little better. Cautiously, she moved it, turning until she could see Adam.

He was sitting in the chair beside her bed and he had fallen asleep. There were streaks of grime down one cheek, and he looked exhausted.

When he wakes, Kirsty thought, with a slow, growing happiness that cancelled out all the pain, I'll tell him that I love him. I'll tell him that the waiting is over for both of us. She lay back against her pillows, content for now to wait until he woke up, and turned to her.

THE END

4 Doctor Nurse Romances
FREE

Coping with the daily tragedies and ordeals of a busy hospital, and sharing the satisfaction of a difficult job well done, people find themselves unexpectedly drawn together. Mills & Boon Doctor Nurse Romances capture perfectly the excitement, the intrigue and the emotions of modern medicine, that so often lead to overwhelming and blissful love. By becoming a regular reader of Mills & Boon Doctor Nurse Romances you can enjoy EIGHT superb new titles every two months plus a whole range of special benefits: your very own personal membership card, a free newsletter packed with recipes, competitions, bargain book offers, plus big cash savings.

AND an Introductory FREE GIFT for YOU.
Turn over the page for details.

**Fill in and send this coupon back today
and we'll send you
4 Introductory
Doctor Nurse Romances yours to keep**

FREE

At the same time we will reserve a
subscription to Mills & Boon
Doctor Nurse Romances for you. Every
two months you will receive the latest
8 new titles, delivered direct to your door.
You don't pay extra for delivery. Postage and
packing is always completely Free.
There is no obligation or commitment –
you receive books only for
as long as you want to.

It's easy! Fill in the coupon below and return it to
**MILLS & BOON READER SERVICE, FREEPOST, P.O. BOX 236,
CROYDON, SURREY CR9 9EL.**

**Please note: READERS IN SOUTH AFRICA write to
Mills & Boon Ltd., Postbag X3010,
Randburg 2125, S. Africa.**

- -

FREE BOOKS CERTIFICATE

**To: Mills & Boon Reader Service, FREEPOST, P.O. Box 236,
Croydon, Surrey CR9 9EL.**

Please send me, free and without obligation, four Dr. Nurse Romances, and reserve a
Reader Service Subscription for me. If I decide to subscribe I shall receive, following my free
parcel of books, eight new Dr. Nurse Romances every two months for £8.00, post and
packing free. If I decide not to subscribe, I shall write to you within 10 days. The free books
are mine to keep in any case. I understand that I may cancel my subscription at any time
simply by writing to you. I am over 18 years of age.
Please write in BLOCK CAPITALS.

Name _____

Address _____

_____

_____ Postcode _____

SEND NO MONEY — TAKE NO RISKS

*Remember, postcodes speed delivery. Offer applies in UK only and is not valid to
present subscribers. Mills & Boon reserve the right to exercise discretion
in granting membership. If price changes are necessary you will be noti-
fied. Offer expires 31st December 1984.*

8DN

EP11□